To Ellie
I hope you love my
dragons like I do.
J.m.m. Adams
Michele

Sophia and the Dragons

Books 1 and 2

By J.M.M. ADAMS

This book may not be reproduced in whole or part by any means without special permission from the Author. This is a work of fiction from the Author's imagination. It does not reflect any living or deceased person. Copyrights reserved.

Copyright © 2019 Dragon Loch Works

All rights reserved.

ISBN: 978-1-393-48638-1

ACKNOWLEDGEMENTS

Cover by: Germancreative on Fivver

Editor: Richard Perfrement

Proof Reader: Rolland E. Wiese

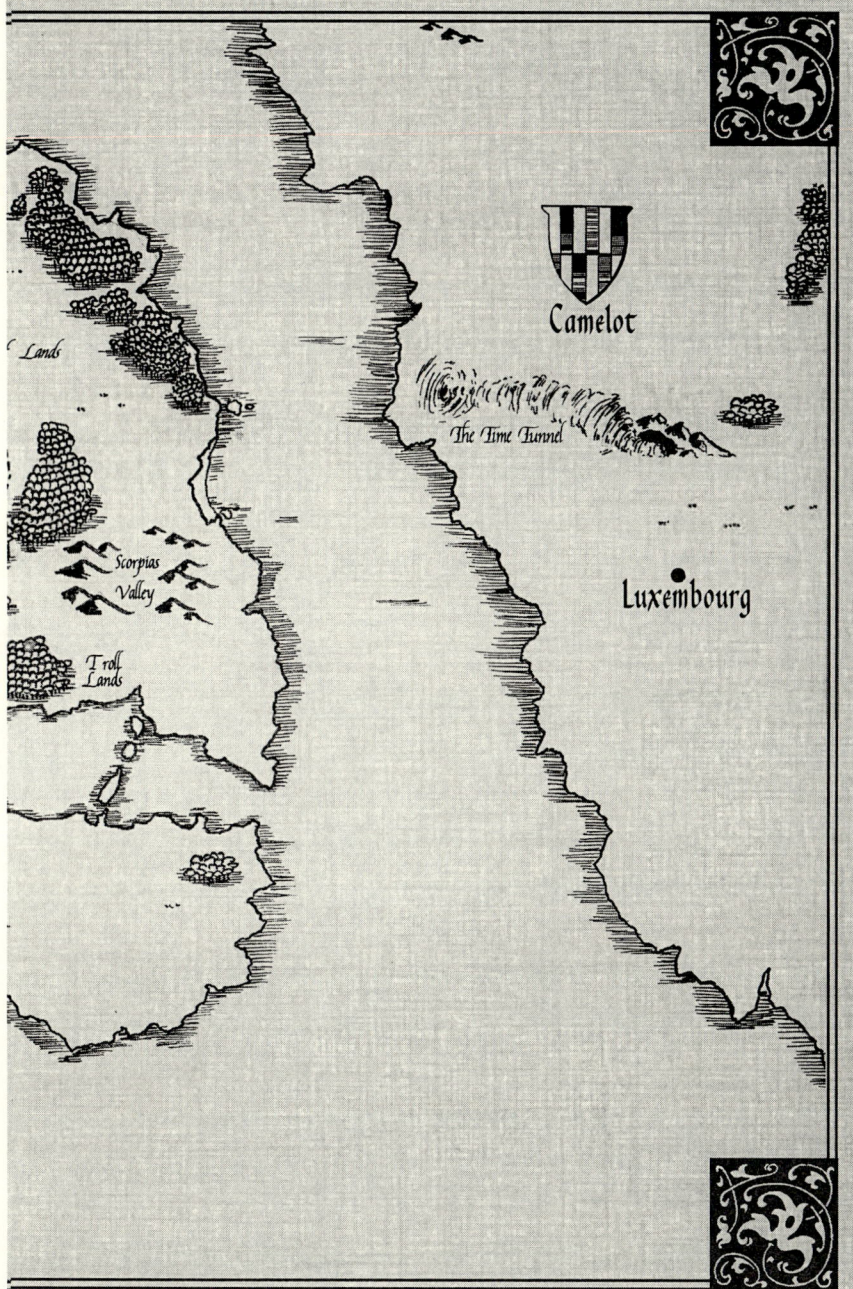

Titles by
JMM Adams

Kanani's Golden Caves

Sophia and the Stradivarius

(Appearing in First String this year at the Indie Film Festivals in Asia, Europe, and World Wide.)

Sophia and the Dragon

The Russian Spy

The Mystery of Sandy Island

The Mystery of St. Moritz

Sophia and the Dragons of L'Azure (2019)

Be sure to check out Michele's other books at

www.dragonlochworks.com

This book is dedicated to all military working dogs

Sophia and the Dragons

Sophia Anderson (From Hawaii, Port Townsend, WA and Luxembourg 2013) Nickname is Sophie.

Kanani (Sophia's long-haired German Shepherd)

John Barnes (Sophia's deceased husband)

Susan and Kimo (Good Friends)

Leila (Sophia's niece)

Jennie (Sophia's sister that disappeared in Egypt through time travel, Leila's mother)

Richard (Jennie's husband that disappeared with her)

Yglais (Mother of Lamorak and Perceval)

Lamorak (Knight of the Round Table, Knight that found Sophia, he was more famous than Gawain.

Perceval (Knight of the Round Table and brother of Lamorak)

Cundrie (Witch, Accolon's wife, cousin to Lamorak and Perceval)

Accalon (Knight of the Round Table and husband to Cundrie)

Bryn (Maid to Sophia in 1180 AD)

Afawen (Maid to Sophia in 1180 AD)

Iago (Page in 1180 AD)

Ivis (The Head Cook at Lamorak's Castle 1180)

Drake (White Dragon)

Meuric –
(Merrick) Wizard

Teyrnon –
Dragon in charge

Albe –
(All + bay) White Dragon

Aedan –
(Born of Fire) Dragon

Gunther –
(Battle Warrior) Dragon, Sophie's Dragon

Drake –
Gunther's young cousin, lives in Camelot

Elwynn –
(Magical fair white being) Dragon

Egan –
(Fire, flame) Dragon

Emmorous – Dragon

Machel – white Dragon

Cham – Machel's little brother, white Dragon

Keeva –
Red Dragon

Female Elves –
Aerin, Faunalyn, Shalendra

Male Elves –
Threwien, Uriodien, Amendel

Dwarves – Gloriddeg Minebreaker, Nubout Leatherjaw,

Andorlir Night-Brew

Eamon – (Aim + an – Guardian of Riches) Prince of

L'Azure -Agalone –

(Son of the King) Older Prince of L'Azure

1

"SOPHIE!" Susan screams as Sophia disappears into the opening of the cave.

"Kanani no! Come back!" Leila called too late. Susan and Leila watch Kanani vanish through the portal.

Sophia tumbled through darkness for a long moment, then landed awkwardly and tumbled to the ground. She didn't know what had happened to her, so she looked around. She was on the ground beside a dirt road; across the road to her right was what looked like an English Pub. There was a bit of haze with the sun shining through and the air was humid, she could feel her hair starting to frizz around her face.

She thought to herself; did I just go through time? This is unbelievable. I thought I could do that in Egypt?

She struggled to her feet only to be knocked down again when Kanani tumbled from the portal, crashing into the back of her knees.

"Kanani, I'm glad to see you too and that you love me so much. I love you even more! Now can you please stop jumping back and forth over me?" She begged her German Shepherd as she struggled to stand back up.

I love you too Sophie, I'm just so happy to see you. Thought Kanani, as she licked Sophie's face.

Sophia stood up and straightened out her jean skirt, dusting off her black t-shirt.

Look out Sophie! There's a strange person approaching us. Kanani was barking warning Sophia.

Sophia heard a horse and looked up. Someone tall rode a big, black stallion towards them. As the rider drew near, Sophia caught the pale glint of sunlight off chain armor. He stopped in front of them and dismounted. He looked in his late twenties, about Sophia's age. He took his helmet off and tucked it under his arm. His long sandy blond hair fell out from under it. He was about six feet tall with a muscular build and the most beautiful blue eyes She had ever seen.

"Stop barking Kanani," Sophia scolded her German Shepherd.

Kanani stopped barking, Ok, Sophie, but he better not hurt us.

"Good day Madam, are you alright?"

"Yes, yes, I think so, thank you for stopping to ask." Sophia stuttered as she continued looking around, still wondering where they were. It looked a lot like Cornwall, but not the Cornwall she was familiar with.

"Who are you?"

"I'm Sophia and this is Kanani, we were exploring caves with my friends and ended up here. May I ask who you are and where I am?"

"Yes, my Lady it is the year of our Lord, 1180, you are in the County of Devon and I am Sir Lamorak de Gales. I am a Knight of the Round Table in King Arthur's court.

"May I pet your animal, Lady?" he asked without waiting for Sophia to answer him. He bent over to pet Kanani.

Sophia was so glad Kanani didn't bite him.

"If she lets you pet her it's ok with me," Sophia managed to say.

I guess if he pets me he's ok Sophie. Kanani wagged her tail.

"I've never seen a dog like this and I have never seen anyone dressed like you." Said Sir Lamorak.

Yeah, we've never seen anyone dressed like you either buddy, Kanani was saying with her tongue hanging out of her mouth.

Sophia's heart was beating so fast she was sure he could hear it.

Here I was dressed like a person from my time, at least I had leggings under my shirt. My hair probably didn't look bad, it was long, dark blonde and braided. Was I really standing here talking to a handsome knight? Sophia thought to herself.

"My dog is an Alsatian," Sophia hoped that would be less confusing than German Shepherd.

"Where are you from?" He asked studying her more closely.

"I'm from Luxembourg. But I'm from the year of our Lord 2013," She whispered.

"Did you say 2013? Did you come here on purpose? I don't understand how that happened." He looked amazed.

"No, it was an accident. I'm lost and really want to go back now!" She was unsure of herself and looked back at the rock she and Kanani apparently came through. The portal was not visible to her now though.

He followed her gaze and apparently saw nothing but a rock either.

Kanani looked too and walked over to the rock sniffing. Yeah, I can't believe we came through that either. Sophie sure does some fun things.

"I do not know how to get you back." He took note of dusk starting to fall. You must come to my Castle, I am not going to let a beautiful young lady and dog stand here all night for thieves to rob and kill."

"Your Castle? I don't have anything proper to put on for a castle visit," She looked down her skirt again, at least she wasn't in shorts!

"I'm sure my mother can find something for you to wear." He said then bent over and gently took her hand, giving it a kiss. Wow, I'll follow you anywhere. Sophia was thinking with a lump in her throat. She was still wondering how she would get back home. She felt a bit of dread in the pit of her stomach as he led her towards his castle.

"Will you remember where you found us?" She asked a bit pleadingly.

"Yes, I will." He turned to look at Sophia, "It's almost dark, and we must hurry."

Sophia grabbed her pack and took Kanani's leash out snapping it on her collar. He walked leading his horse behind them.

Would Susan and Leila get Kimo and come find us? Oh, I shouldn't have listened to Leila and I should have stayed home working on Grandpa's notes in my library in Luxembourg.

Sophia was choking back tears. She was having a hard time letting go since John, her husband, had been killed almost a year ago.

"What is that you have on your dog?" He interrupted Sophia's self-pity.

"It's called a leash; I don't think it's invented yet."

"No, it isn't, I have a lot of questions for you. Don't worry. You will be safe in my care, my Lady."

"I hope so," Sophia answered down cast.

We'll be ok Sophie, he's ok and I'm here with you. Kanani was walking close to Sophie and looking up at her.

As they advanced down the road Sophia looked around, the countryside was green with rolling hills. She decided to try and enjoy her predicament, since she was on this adventure whether She wanted to be or not.

I don't have anything to worry about. Susan and Kimo will take care of Leila and the house in Luxembourg. It is so beautiful here and looks very different from how I remembered it when Jennie and I came here on summer vacations with our Grandma and Grandpa. The farms and roads weren't here now, it was untouched. Being summer, the weather was nice and Kanani didn't seem upset by our recent experience. So, I might as well enjoy my adventure. It would be something else to write about when I got home. Sophia was telling herself.

After walking for about an hour Lamorak pointed at a castle and said with pride in his voice. "There's my castle."

"Wow, it's gorgeous!" Sophia was getting excited forgetting her predicament. She was a bit anxious to meet his family though.

"She has been in my family many years. When my father was slain in battle it became mine, which was five years ago. I now take care of my mother, Lady Yglais." He looked thoughtful.

"I don't think it's a good idea for anyone to know where you have come from, at least not today. My mother will wonder if she sees the way you are dressed. I will put you into a spare bedchamber right away, and then go find her. I will mention I met you, but not tell Her where you came from."

He was still talking, but he lost Sophia's attention, because they had just entered the most magnificent castle she had ever seen! They were walking through the courtyard no one was about.

She followed him into the stables. He handed his horse over to a page. The page looked at Sophia with suspicion but didn't say anything.

"Oh, he gives me the chills, he is staring at me Sir Lamorak."

"Never mind him. Come let's get you and your dog into the castle."

He pushed her gently in front of him to leave the stable. Then Kanani and Sophia followed Lamorak into the main hall of the castle. She tried looking around at everything without tripping, but had a hard time, because He was moving her rapidly to their room. They got there and He opened up the doors.

"This will be your chamber, please go in quickly." Lamorak told her.

She looked around at the beautiful room; there was a bed, washstand and a window looking out over the moors.

Yahoo, this is a neat pad Sophie. Check out that bed! Kanani bounded into to the room jumping on the bed, and then jumped off.

"Well your dog likes the room," laughed Lamorak.

"Make yourself comfortable and I will have some dresses and clothing brought in for you, my Lady. Don't be frightened, are you?"

"Not so much frightened, as concerned if I will be accepted. Then there's that little thing about how long I'll be here." She pinched herself, yep, she was awake, and this was not a dream. He saw her pinching herself.

"I don't understand how you got here, but everything will work out. I am pleased that I was the one that found you. This will put some excitement into our lives," he said with a bid of glee in his voice, and then he grinned turning around to walk out the door. He stopped remembering something, turned back to her around said; "I will escort you to dinner in two hours."

"Great, thank you."

Then he closed the door and disappeared.

"Doesn't he suspect I were going to try and get back home?" She said to Kanani as she took off her backpack and looked inside to see what Susan had loaded into it that morning.

No, I don't think so Sophie, but don't worry this is fun. Kanani looked in the bag with Sophia. She found the phone Grandpa had given her for the planned time travel in Egypt.

She had planned on going back in time to try to find her sister and brother -in -law. Jennie had disappeared over a year ago while on an excavation trip with her husband and Leila. Leila had stayed behind in the camp that morning. They never returned to her. That's how Leila had come to live in Luxembourg under phone worked for time travel; well she was going to give it a test after getting cleaned up. She felt and looked grubby and dirty. She walked over to the basin of water and washed her face, then looked into the mirror sighing. Of course, she had no makeup in her pack. She was going to miss a lot of things. A knock at the door startled her.

"Come in."

The door opened, and a young maid walked in carrying ten gowns, then another one followed her carrying more clothes. They were gorgeous gowns; Sophia couldn't believe it!

"Look at those dresses! I am so thankful; I don't know what to say except thank you."

"You're very welcome Lady," said the first maid. "I will hang them up in the closet; do you need anything else or help with anything my Lady?"

"Yes, I need to know what to wear to dinner tonight, and I need some face stuff to make me pretty."

"Afawen," she pointed to the other girl, "put some makeup over there for you by the basin, if you need other colors let me know. There is also some lotion with it, would you like some hot water to be brought in for a bath?"

"I would love that so much!" Exclaimed Sophia.

"Ok, my name is Bryn and we will be back soon," but instead of leaving she walked over to the hanging gowns and pulled one out. "This blue one would look very nice on you tonight." She said holding it up for inspection.

It was the most gorgeous blue gown Sophia had ever seen. "Thank you. That one will do fine. It's nice to meet you Bryn.

My name is Sophia; my friends call me Sophie."

"Your welcome, I will be here to assist you for your stay. Then she giggled, looking down at Kanani. May I pet her? She's so pretty."

"Yes, let me introduce you to Kanani." Sophia walked over and knelt by her dog, then invited Bryn to come over and pet her.

"Thank you, my Lady," then she stood up. "I'll be back with your hot water very soon." She turned and walked out of the room.

"What an endearing young lady." Sophia said to Kanani and then sighed, "This might be fun, I'm going to try and call Grandpa."

Kanani was looking around the room and thinking, Not bad for a place to stay. I wonder where we are? Yes, Sophie, this will be fun, Woof woof!

Sophia knew that Susan and Leila were probably frantic that she and Kanani had disappeared.

Picking up the phone She dialed the number Grandpa had given her. It rang only once to her great relief. She heard his voice on the other end of it.

"Hello. Sophie is this you my dear?"

"Hi Grandpa. Yes, it's me and I want you to know that I am ok and it's so nice to hear your voice!"

"It's nice to hear your voice too, my dear. Susan and Kimo called telling me about your disappearance right after it happened. They were very upset, but I calmed them down. We'll figure out how to get you home. What year did you land in sweetheart?"

"I landed in 1180 and I'm staying at Sir Lamorak de Gales castle in Devon, England. He is a knight in King Arthur's court, can you Google him Grandpa, and let me know whatever you can find out about him?" She pleaded.

"Yes, dear I can do that for you. Are they treating you like the princess you are to me?" The warmth in his voice quieted her.

"Yes, Grandpa they are; I have ten beautiful gowns hanging in my wardrobe! Lamorak acts like I'm here to stay forever!"

"Well, sweetheart this is good for you to have a little adventure. I want you to start living again after your heartache of losing John," he told her endearingly.

"I know Grandpa, but this is strange, oh, someone is knocking on my door; I'll call you back tomorrow. Please let everyone know I'm ok. I love you Grandpa."

"Ok, sweetheart I will, and I love you too," then he hung up.

Sophia tossed the phone in her pack and hurried over to open the door. The castle attendants were carrying her bath water, soap and anything else she needed. They filled the tub and as they were leaving Bryn walked in.

"Well it looks in place, my Lady. Can I be of help with your bath or help you dress?"

"Yes, could you come back in thirty minutes and help me with the dress? I would be grateful."

"Yes, I can, now enjoy your hot bath my Lady and I will be back soon." Bryn left closing the door behind her.

"I will," shouted Sophia after her.

It looked like a lovely bath, Sophia peeled off her dirty clothes, folding them and placing them in her pack. Then she stepped into the hot inviting bath. It felt good on her aching muscles and she relaxed. Not having much time, because Bryn would be back soon, she got out and dried off. She was just slipping the dress on when there was a knock on the door.

"Bryn, is that you?"

"Yes, my lady. May I come in now?" She asked.

"Yes, I'm ready for you."

She entered and asked, "How was your bath?"

"Fantastic! It picked up my spirit and I needed that."

"Good," she helped button up the dress and apply face color. When they were all done Bryn looked at her.

"You look lovely, my Lady. Yes, you will do."

"Really? Thank you so much!" Sophia gave Bryn a hug, which made her blush.

"I will make sure Kanani is fed, what does she eat?" Bryn asked.

Well, as long as she feeds me what I like, come on Sophie, tell her what I like to eat. Kanani was thumping her tail at Bryn.

"She can eat meat and needs drinking water. I would really appreciate that, thank you." Sophia said.

"Your welcome, I'll be back after you go to dinner and take care of her."

"Thank you again Bryn," then she left. Sophia hugged Kanani; she just cocked her and gave Sophia a look.

"We're going to be ok, sweetie. Bryn will come back with your food and take you out for potty. I love you Nani!" Sophia buried her face into Kanani's neck.

I love you too, don't be gone too long. Kanani didn't want her to leave at all.

Then there was a knock on the door, letting go of Kanani Sophia walked over and opened it up. Handsome Sir Lamorak was standing there!

"Good evening," Sophia said, "do you like how I look now?" She asked him to twirl around.

Then she really looked at him, he was so handsome in his blue linen shirt and black pants. The blue shirt brought out the blue of his eyes. Oh, she could fall for him.

"You are very beautiful my Lady," he replied, "I am honored to escort you to dinner." Then he stuck out his arm for Sophia to take hold of. She looked back at Kanani and told her to be a good girl. That she would be back soon. Sophia was really nervous.

They walked into the dining room. Everyone was already seated.

"Mother, I would like to introduce you to Lady Sophia of Luxembourg," Lamorak stepped back to show off Sophia and introduce her to his mother. She was shocked he called her that, how was she going to pull this one off?

"Very nice to meet you Lady Yglais," she said with a curtsy.

"It's very nice to meet you as well, let me introduce you to everyone, my dear." Lady Yglais continued. She pointed as she spoke, "The man to my left is my other son, Perceval; next to him is Accalon and then his wife Cundrie. Accalon is my nephew and both he and his wife are staying here with us for the time being. Why don't you sit here next to me on my right, dear?" She patted the seat next to her.

"Hello, it's nice to meet all of you," Sophia said, then turned to Yglais, Lamorak's mother, "I am honored to sit next to you my Lady, thank you."

Lamorak pulled out the chair and she sat down. Sophia made it through dinner without any mishaps. Stories were told about the quests the knights had been on. Then she heard about how King Arthur had called everyone into his Kingdom for a festival starting tomorrow. Cundrie talked about what clothes to pack, Lady Yglais said that everyone should get up early, because the wagons needed to be packed up. Lady Yglais told Sophia that she was invited to go with them. Then the conversation changed and she asked Sophia if she loved children. Sophia told her yes, that she wanted to open a school someday. Lady Yglais thought that was a great idea. Sophia didn't mean for her to think she was opening one here! They talked about that for a while. After dinner was over the Page, Iago came in and gestured for Cundrie to leave and talk to him. Sophia wondered what that was about. No one else seemed to bother about it, so Sophia let it go.

Lamorak and his mother walked Sophia back to her room talking about what she needed to take for the trip to Camelot.

Sophia was a bit anxious how Kanani had done without her. She opened the door to her room, turned to say goodnight and thanked both of them for the lovely evening.

"I'll see you early in the morning, goodnight kind sir."

"Good night Lady Yglais, thank you for your hospitality."

"Good night my Lady," Lamorak and his mother both said, then they turned to walk away.

Sophia closed the door and screamed!!!!

2

THEY HEARD HER and Lamorak and ran back to Sophia's room. He thrust the door open and grabbed ahold of Sophia. Looking around he saw what she was so upset about.

"Who did this?" Sophia cried, running over to her backpack. She started throwing everything out; my phone is missing!!!! All of my lovely dresses have been slashed, but that was nothing compared to losing my phone." Sophia was devastated.

"I have a pretty good idea," said Lamorak angrily.

Bryn walked in with Kanani. Kanani ran over and jumped up on Sophia crying.

It's ok; really don't' cry. I'm here for you. Kanani started kissing Sophia.

"Thank you Kanani." Sophie sniffled.

"What happened? We were just here half an hour ago! This is horrible! Let me go get some help and we will get this cleaned up for you, my Lady." Then Bryn ran out of the room.

"Thank you," Sophia called after her as she sat down on her bed, she was upset.

"How can we ever get in touch with Grandpa again Kanani?" Sophia talked to her dog.

You have me; we have each other. Kanani kissed her again.

After everything was cleaned up, Lamorak insisted on sleeping outside the door of her chambers that evening to make her feel safe.

"Remember, Sophia, we go to Camelot tomorrow and you have traveled along way today. You need to feel safe tonight. Try and sleep." Then he closed the door and sat down on his cot to get comfortable for the night. *If I could just survive until that time, I would be happy.*

Sophia slept fitfully, tossing and turning. she couldn't believe this was happening to her. Maybe when she woke up, she'd be back home in her own bed. Perhaps this was a bad dream. At least Kanani was here snuggling up to her.

3

THE NEXT MORNING Lamorak was up before Sophia and had taken Kanani out for a walk.

Thank goodness Lamorak heard me whining at the door to go out. Then he took me into the big kitchen and the ladies fed me. Thought, Kanani.

Sophia was up and dressed in the only dress not shredded when he came back.

"Good Morning Sophia, how are you this morning?"

"I'm fine and ready to go to Camelot, how are you?" Sophia asked going over and hugging Kanani.

"Me too, my mother found some more dresses for you, so we are all packed. Here is something for you to eat," he said.

Bryn walked in and placed a tray of cheese and crackers on Sophia's small round oak table placed under the window.

"Kanani and I already ate. You don't have much in here to take, but let Bryn help you after you eat."

"Thank you," she said to Bryn and Lamorak both, sitting down and taking a bite. She tossed Kanani a cracker.

That's nice! How about a second one?

"Kanani, stop begging young lady!" Lamorak said sternly.

Darn, he won't be easy to fool.

When she was full they helped her pack, they left the room and Lamorak loaded her things into the carriage.

"You are riding with my Mother and Cundrie, then Bryn and Afawen will be in the carriage behind you. Don't give Cundrie any information. She is a witch or thinks she is; I think she had something to do with ransacking your room last night. She is on to you somehow and it enrages her not knowing how you got here." Lamorak warned Sophia.

"Kanani and I will be our best behavior," she told him with a grin, then mounted the steps to the carriage with Kanani on her heels.

No way is Sophie going without me. Kanani was not letting Sophie out of her site!

Lamorak just cracked a smile and shook his head. He had never met a woman like this before; it was a challenge for him.

Sophia thought it was exciting looking out the window watching the horses ahead of them, then looking back seeing Lamorak, Perceval and Accalon in full armor riding their horses dressed in Camelot colors.

Yglais was knitting and Cundrie was staring out the window not paying any attention to either of them. Sophia hoped it stayed like that. Kanani was on the floor by Sophia's feet. The ladies only made a small fuss about having a dog in the carriage, actually Yglais was fine with it, Cundrie was the one that voiced her opinion. Finally, Yglais started talking to Sophia not looking up from her project.

"Lady Sophia, we can talk about the school now that we have some time. There are many children of different ages around us with no one to give them proper instruction. What will you need to get started?" Yglais asked her. The night before they had discussed opening a school.

"Well I need something to write on to teach them the alphabet so they will be able to read. For the younger children I have a more hands on way of teaching." Sophia answered her.

"Cundrie you can get something for Sophia to start teaching, I want you to be VERY helpful to her and not give her any grief." Stated Yglais sternly looking up in Cundrie's direction.

"Hmm," said Cundrie looking up at her. I apologize I was daydreaming and didn't hear what you two were talking about. Would you mind repeating the conversation?"

Boy Sophie don't trust that person. I'm going to have to watch Cundrie. Kanani stared at Cundrie.

Yglais shook her head in disgust and repeated what they had just discussed.

"I'm sure I can find all of the supplies you need. I'll work on it at Camelot," she said then looked back out the window.

Sophia wondered if Cundrie was thinking about her phone and how to find out where she was from. Arriving at Camelot their carriages stopped, looking out Sophia saw they had a vacant place to camp.

"Sophia, you and Kanani can wander around, but be back in one hour. The men will put up tents, I've been told Camelot is too full and we'll have to camp out here. So we will unpack and settle in after the tents are ready. Have fun," Yglais told her.

"I will, thank you," Sophia said standing up and jumping out with Kanani.

"You stick by my side, Kanani and no snatching food from anyone young lady," Sophia realized a leash was not an option here. She didn't want to do anything to draw attention herself.

Sophie, this is fun, but I'm a bit afraid of getting lost. I won't leave your side, I promise. Oh, smell all of that good food. This might be hard not to get a bite along the way.

She was amazed at all of the people, the food being put out, tents being raised and people, kids everywhere. Before she knew it, her hour was up.

"Darn, I'm going to be late we had better start back Kanani." She turned around quickly and bummed into a Knight. UMPH!

"I'm sorry, I wasn't looking where I was going." She told him gathering her composure.

"Sophia!" Exclaimed the Knight.

4

SOPHIA LOOKED up to see who knew her name and couldn't believe her eyes!

"Richard! Where's Jennie?" Sophia asked him. He was her brother-in-law that had disappeared with her sister in Egypt some time ago.

"She's back at our tent, come on she won't believe this." He said excitedly taking her hand and pulling her in the direction of his tent.

"How did you get here?" He asked looking back at Sophia again. "Hi Kanani," he said looking at her.

Hey, Richard nice seeing you. Kanani thumped her tail.

"I'd like to ask you the same thing," Sophia answered.

"Here we are, we'll exchange stories when we get Jennie's attention."

Then he stopped in front of a woman. Sophia couldn't believe it was her big sister Jennie.

"Jennie, look what I brought you home," he said.

"Now what did my handsome Knight bring me?" she asked him playfully turning around.

Jennie screamed, dropped the dish of food she was preparing and ran over hugging Sophia so tight she didn't think she could breathe. Kanani was jumping on Jennie trying to get her attention too.

"My Sophia, how did you get here? Where's Leila?" she asked her.

"Leila is home in Luxembourg and Kanani and I are here by accident." Sophia told her. "Sir Lamorak found me and I'm staying with him and his family. I've been here only a short time."

"Well it's amazing to find you here! Hi, Kanani you came with Sophia too I see. Good girl," Jennie rubbed Kanani's ears.

I like that!

"Sophia!" She heard her name and looked around. She saw Lamorak walking her way looking for her.

"I'm over here!" Sophia shouted loud enough for him to hear her over all the noise. Lamorak walked over to her.

"Hi, I'm sorry I didn't make it back but I ran into my Sister and Brother-In-Law. Let me introduce you." Sophia said taking his hand and introducing him to her family.

"Does everyone time travel in your family?" He asked shaking their hands.

"No, just my family." Sophia said laughing. She was thrilled to have her sister back into her life again.

"Tonight, is free time, let me go tell my family we ran into Sophia's family. I will be back with some food and drink then we can talk. Don't start telling any good tales without me," he turned hurrying off into the direction of their camp.

"Ok, we won't, hurry back," Sophia called after him.

"Sophia he's handsome! I think he likes you." Jennie said.

"I know but, it hasn't been that long since I lost John," she replied.

"What do you mean, you lost John?" Jennie was shocked. "What happened, did he leave you?"

"No, he was killed in a rescue mission. I'll tell you about it later. He was a good man and good to me, I miss him terribly." Sophia told her getting misty eyed.

"Oh Sophie, I'm so sorry, I didn't know," Jennie was sad for her. "I want you to know something about history regarding Lamorak. He supposedly was in love with a lady from a distant place. She left him and he was so devastated he never married and ended up getting killed looking for the Holy Grail a short time after she left him." I found this years ago when I was studying King Arthur for deposition when I went for my Doctorate. Maybe that was you! You have the ability to change all of that." Jennie said earnestly.

"Wow," Sophia was speechless. "Shh, here comes Lamorak now."

"Is Leila alright, is she here too?" Asked Jennie.

"No, she's not here. You weren't listening and yes she is alright. Leila is the reason I'm here, she insisted on going caving. She's back in Luxembourg with Susan and Kimo." Sophia answered.

Jennie was holding her hand as Lamorak walked up to them. He had a servant following him with a tray of good smelling food.

"Is it alright to place this tray here?" Lamorak asked Jennie.

"Yes, that's fine, let me make room for it. How nice of you to feed us tonight Lamorak." Sophia told him.

"No problem at all, I get to spend the evening with my favorite Lady and learn more about her from her sister. What more could I ask for?" He was grinning from ear to ear like a little boy.

Sophia could picture him as child getting his way with everyone with that boyish grin and good humor.

"Your favorite lady?" Sophia asked.

"Did I say that? Yes, I believe I did say that my Lady!" He then bowed in front of her. "You look so lovely this evening Lady Sophia, may I be so honored as to sit next to you?"

"How could I resist your request my Lord and Knight!" She answered bowing back at him laughing.

"Well then let us all sit down and begin," Lamorak had his servant pour us some delicious red wine.

"I would like to know all about you, Lady Sophia," Lamorak took her hand and kissed it.

"I will do my best kind Sir. Jennie and I grew up moving all over the world as children. We lived with our mother in Hawaii when our father was killed in the Vietnam War. Shortly afterwards our mother died from a broken heart. Jennie and I were little so our father's grandparents took us in. Grandpa was a spy during the cold war for the United State Government. Then he worked co-op missions on special assignments. We lived in Luxembourg as children with them. That is where I was living before, I came here, in grandfather's house. Now I know you are wondering what is the Viet Nam war, what is a co-op mission, I will explain that at another time."

"Please continue I am very interested." Lamorak answered.

"I ended up moving over to Maui when I turned twenty and that's where Kanani was born.

Kanani heard her name and perked up.

I love to hear stories about me.

"From there I had enough money from our father's estate to buy a small market in Lanai. John, my deceased husband, was a retired Ranger with Special Forces when I met him a long time ago. Kanani and I had a previous adventure on Maui, so the F.B.I. was called in. John did work for them too and that is how we first met. He retired and bought a small boutique hotel on Lanai to be near me. I was not aware that I had bought a hot property though. There was a map hidden in the storeroom of the market, which showed where smugglers were storing diamonds, and gold for shipment out of caves on Lanai and Molokai. Jennie and Richard's daughter Leila, Kanani, my friend Susan, and I were caught up in the middle of capturing them. My shop was torched and my yacht was totaled, then John asked me to marry him. Our friends, Susan and Kimo joined us in a double ceremony. Then we bought houses in Port Townsend, WA. Which led us into another crazy adventure. It started with the antique shop I owned. A woman came into my shop one evening towards closing. She brought me a mysterious violin from our grandfather. That violin took all of us on an adventure through France, Germany and Luxembourg. After the case was solved, we ended up with Grandpa's house in Luxembourg, so

Susan, Kimo, John, Kanani, and I moved there. Grandpa also left a lot of money for Jennie and myself." Sophia looked at her sister. Jennie's eyes were as round as saucers with astonishment.

"Jennie, we have a lot of money in a bank for us to use, I got the house in Luxembourg and the Stradivarius." She looked at Jennie, "Can you handle me continuing?"

"Yes! Yes please go on, I'm listening. What happened to grandpa?" Jennie asked.

"Well, grandfather is in a monastery near Luxembourg and he told me briefly something we didn't know about our ancestry. Our last name is not Anderson, Jennie, it's Stradivarius!"

At that Jennie jumped up from the table knocking her plate of food onto the ground.

"Oh, I'm so sorry," she said. "Let me clean it up." Then she got up and grabbed a rag.

"No, sit," said Richard, "Sophie, please continue dear I can't wait to hear the rest of this tale!"

The servant took the rag out of Jennie's hand and cleaned up the mess as Sophia continued.

"I got a call from Leila in Egypt! She was at the Consulate and told me of her ordeal with the two of you vanishing on her. I had her flown to Luxembourg, that's where we picked her up and took her to Echternach. Then John and Kimo went back to Port Townsend to settle affairs and sell my shop, I took Leila, Susan, and Kanani to Egypt to see if we could find the two of you. We found the door you went through and Kanani and I found your notes left for Leila. I ended up here because Leila wanted to go caving in

Luxembourg. We bought tickets for Egypt the following week, we were going back to go through time and look for you guys. You see, I lost John a year ago, there was never a body, but his chopper went down when he opted in a mission to go in and save some woman and children in Afghanistan. Grandpa wanted me to have something to do to take my mind off the loss of John."

"Oh, Sophia I am so sorry," said Richard grabbing her hand.

"It's ok, Richard, thank you. I'm getting over it." she said.

"How did he die on a mission if he was retired? What happened Sophia?" asked Richard.

"He was asked to re-enlist just for a special mission. The first trip in went well, and then they went back. Their helicopter was shot down and they could find no survivors. Finally, the military had the funerals with no bodies in D. C. There was a 21-gun salute using artillery and battery pieces. There were bagpipers too playing Amazing Grace. All of us widows were given medals and flags. Then an envelope was given to the other widows. I could see the look of amazement and joy when they opened them. It was money I arranged for them to have to help with expenses now that they were on their own. It was the least I could do." Sophia finished and looked around and everyone one was sitting there in disbelief.

So, after a time she continued. "Grandpa is a bit of an inventor and he gave me a phone that will work through time. Lucky for me Susan packed the phone, because the next thing I knew I fell through a secret door with Kanani landing on top of me; that is when Lamorak found us."

"Then things started happening to me and my phone was stolen at

Lamorak's, I came here with him and that is when I ran into you. That's the short version." She took a deep breath and asked, "Shouldn't we go back and get Leila? I gather the two of you want to stay in this time?"

"Yes, if we can get Leila to come back with us we'll stay," Jennie told me taking a bite of food off her new plate the servant put down in front of her.

"What a tale," Lamorak added.

"Yes, great story, Sophie," Richard said taking a drink of his wine.

"What do we do now?" Sophia asked.

5

"THAT IS something we will have to think about Sophia. In the meantime, I would like to tell you a bit about myself." Lamorak continued but Jennie interrupted him.

"I don't want to seem rude, Lamorak. Your life is very interesting; I have read all about you in history books. Sophia would love to hear about it later, but it sounds like someone has Sophie's phone, this is very dangerous. Someone could misuse this evidence and find their way into the future from Camelot. It could be dangerous."

"I don't think you are rude my Lady; I have to agree with you. I have a pretty good idea who has the phone. That will be your mission and Sophia's to find the thief while Richard and I are meeting King Arthur at the Round Table day after tomorrow. Both of you have two weeks to find out, then Richard and I will take care of the problem." Lamorak said with determination.

"Ok, I take the challenge how about you Sophie?" Jennie asked her.

"Yes, I take the challenge, but I still want the short version of your life Lamorak." She replied.

"That I will give to you sometime when we are sitting by the camp fire my

Lady," he said gallantly looking at her gently.

"Ok, I'll have to accept that. So, for the next two weeks my sister and I will play detective then we will decide our fate from there, it a fair plan I can live with." Sophia told everyone, feeling pleased with the situation.

"This has been a pleasant evening, we should really be getting back Sophia, we can meet both of you after breakfast back here," Lamorak told Richard and Jennie standing up.

No, I don't want to leave Richard I like being here. Oh, ok, if you say it's ok Sophie I'll get out of my comfortable spot and follow you.

"It's been a terrific evening!" Sophia chimed in.

"I agree," said Richard standing up.

"It's been a great blessing to have found you Sophie. Thank you for the wonderful evening," my sister said wrapping her arms around her again.

"Ok girls you can be together all day tomorrow, let's go Sophia." Lamorak shook Richards hand and turned towards her.

"Ok Lamorak I'm coming with you, just a minute." Before letting go of Jennie she kissed her on the cheek, Lamorak took her hand and led her away with the servant following behind.

Sophia kept looking back until they were out of site.

"Where am I sleeping tonight, Lamorak?"

"Sophia, I have you in a small room inside the big tent, I am sleeping in the main chamber to make sure you and Kanani are safe from Cundrie and her witch craft. Plus, anyone else trying to scare you away and find out your secret."

"Thank you, I can sleep peacefully tonight. The first time in a long time."

When they arrived back at Lamorak's camp, Perceval was standing by the fire, Accalon was there and they were talking. Yglais was getting up to go to sleep.

"There you two are," Yglais said, "I hope you had a nice time visiting with your sister, Lady Sophia."

"Yes, I did, thank you for not minding Lamorak spending time with us tonight."

"That's fine, Lamorak can do what he wants. Good night you too." Then she walked to her tent.

"Good night Lady," Sophia said.

"Good night, Mother." Then Lamorak looked at her.

"Let me escort you and Kanani to your chambers."

"Ok, I'm beat. Come on Kanani." Kanani followed Sophia into the tent.

With that Sophia retired for the night and so did Kanani and Lamorak.

She lay down and thought of all the things that had transpired. Did she really want to go back to the future? She knew she had too at least for a while. Could she ever get back home and ever find her way back here? Sophia could stop Lamorak from getting murdered at such a young age. Sophia just couldn't solve everything in her mind; She would have to see what tomorrow would bring. With that thought she was out for the night. Kanani was laying on her feet sound asleep as well.

Sophia felt Kanani licking her and woke up. Sophie, I hear noises outside.

She listened, there was something going on outside. She decided they were safe where they were, rubbed Kanani's face and turned on her side going back over to sleep. The next morning Kanani woke her up early. She got up and put on a blue dress, fixed her hair and peeked out her door. Lamorak was fast asleep in the common area.

"Kanani be quiet," Sophia placed her finger over her mouth and motioned for her to listen. They tip toed past him and got outside without being heard. Sophia craved a cup of coffee; maybe her sister had some? Calling Kanani softly they made their way to her place. Jennie was already up fixing breakfast and was delighted to see them.

I had to go potty and I'm hungry, it's good to be up early. Kanani wagged her tail.

"Good morning little sister, did you sleep well?"

"Yes, I did, you don't have any coffee, do you?" Sophia asked hopefully.

Jennie looked at her grinning, "Do you really think I wouldn't pack everything I could for this adventure? Of course, I have coffee, let me pour you a cup."

"Really? Thank you so much," Sophia exclaimed as she picked up the warm cup and savored the smell.

"Hmmm, this is heaven. I can't remember being this happy, even with all this turmoil right now in my life."

"I know what you mean, I have to get Leila though. It was so hard not having her during the African adventure, but at least she was with you. Now she isn't with either one of us, I hope she's ok!"

"Don't worry Jennie, we'll get her soon. She loves Kimo and Susan, they are family to her just as they are to me." Sophia put an arm around Jennie and kissed her cheek.

Jennie wiped tears from her eyes and said, "Would you like some breakfast?"

"Yes please, Kanani would too, thank you," Sophia said as she handed her a plate for Kanani; then for herself.

That's good. Kanani gobbled up the scrambled eggs, licked her dish and brought it back over to Jennie placing it down in front of her.

"That's cute Kanani, but you'll have to wait for lunch." Jennie laughingly said as she carried her own plate and coffee joining Sophie around the fireplace and ate in silence.

"There you are!" Exclaimed Lamorak walking over to them. "I knew I'd find you here. Ummm, what are you drinking?"

"It's coffee, here have a taste." Sophia said as she handed him the cup.

"This is good; another modern convenience I presume?" he asked.

"Of course, keep that and I'll get another cup." Sophia stood up to get another cup.

"How about some breakfast?" Jennie asked Lamorak.

"Yes please," He said sitting down next to Sophia's chair. "Where's Richard this morning?"

"He had an errand to do. Oh, look there he is now," Jennie pointed at Richard making his way over to them.

"Good morning everyone," He walked over kissed Jennie and handed her some herbs.

"Good morning Richard," both Lamorak and Sophia said together. She looked at him and they both laughed.

"Thank you for the herbs dear," Jennie was ecstatic.

"You are very welcome, I can show you where in the woods I got them so that you and Sophie can get some more."

"Fantastic," answered Jennie.

"What are doing with them Jennie?" Sophia asked her.

"I'm using some for cooking and others for making ointments to put on Richard when he comes home cut and bleeding from his Knightly duties." She said looking at Richard and smiling.

"Well I have a lot to learn, plus we have to try and see if Cundrie took my phone and find out what she plans on doing with it." Sophia added.

"That's right," said Lamorak," it could be dangerous if she found her way to your world. If she got back to our time, she would be a greater threat than Morgan Le Fay!"

"Unless they team up and go together!" Sophia exclaimed.

"Ok it's settled then. After breakfast little sister we are going to check out different merchants and keep our ears open." Jennie said.

"Deal," Sophia replied getting up to help clean the dishes.

"Wait! Richard and I are free today, we can tour Camelot together, I planned on introducing you, Sophia to Guinevere and King Arthur. We have been invited to dinner with them and I'm sure they can make space for two more, so Richard and Jennie you are invited to come along with us today."

"That's wonderful," exclaimed Jennie. "Let me put on a prettier dress, Sophie let's change your clothes too and I'll put some makeup on you. Can you Knights give us an hour?"

"We certainly can, I have some things to attend too, I will be back in a hour," said Lamorak bowing and kissing Sophia's hand. Then he turned to leave but remembered something. "Richard why don't you come with me."

"Don't mind if I do, bye ladies," he said mischievously walking off with Lamorak.

"Ok, Sophie, let's get started."

"Great idea, do you have a lot of dresses?" Sophia asked her.

"Plenty, come take a look."

With that Sophia followed Jennie into her tent and Kanani followed behind jumping on Jennie's bed. Jennie just smiled and shook her head.

"Jennie how did you end up in King Arthurs time entering through Egypt? I've been thinking about it, but can't make any sense out of it."

"There were three doors, in Egypt after we entered the main door. We tried one time period and ended up with dinosaurs chasing us, so we left. We couldn't get back out the main door so we tried another portal; this one was the Civil War age! We left that in a hurry too going through the remaining portal and hoping this one would lead us to something better. It did, it was this time and we fell deeply in love with it. The only problem was that we couldn't get home to Leila. Does that help you understand a bit more?" Jeannie asked her.

"Yes, sister it does." Sophia told her turning back to find a dress she liked. Luckily, they were the same size, her sister was still slender and very pretty with her dark curly hair falling down to her waist.

6

THE MEN returned suddenly, luckily, they were dressed and ready to go. Richard popped his head into the tent.

"Jennie?" He asked.

"Yes, sweetheart we're ready, why are you guys back so soon?" Jennie asked.

"We'll explain as soon as you two are ready and come out to join us," he said, closing the tent flap and returning back to talk to Lamorak.

"Wow you are so pretty Lady Sophie," Lamorak exclaimed, as Sophia emerged from the tent in a lavender skirt falling to her ankles and a plain white top. Her sister had put Sophia's long curly dark blond hair up in a bun with strands of hair falling down around her face. Sophia felt like it made her look softer.

"Thank you, kind sir," Sophia answered bowing to him with a grin.

Then Jennie walked out and Richard came over to put his arm around his pretty wife kissing her head. He was six feet tall, Jennie and Sophia weren't short, but looked short next to these two knights.

"What's the news?" Sophia wanted to know looking at both men.

"Dinner is still on, but I saw Cundrie and Morgan Le Fay talking yesterday, and found out today that they disappeared, Guinevere is gone too. The King wants to have dinner as planned, but I bet Morgan, Cundrie and Guinevere found out about you and are trying to find the opening! We need to discuss a journey back to the future and find out what they are up to. Then bring them back as soon as possible." Sir Lamorak said.

Richard agreed.

"Wow that's huge, how is King Arthur taking it?" Sophia asked.

"We'll find out tonight my dear," said Richard. With that they decided to enjoy the day anyway.

"Be a good girl and stay here Kanani. We will be back to check on you later. I love you." Sophia bent over and rubbed her dog on the head.

I don't want to stay. Can't I go to the castle too?

Sophie felt bad leaving Kanani but put her in Jennie's tent and closed the entry door.

They walked through all of the vendor tents, eating, and then took a walk through the forest gathering more herbs. After they took them back to Sophia's sisters' tent. From there they walked over and into the inner court of Camelot.

"This nothing like I imagined," Sophia said looking around.

"Me either," Jennie said with her mouth open in awe.

"Hey, how did Richard become a Knight with Arthur?" Sophia whispered to Jennie.

"We arrived some time ago and there were tryouts for being a Knight, but not a Knight of The Round Table. Richard amazed himself and me too by doing so well, they knighted him right away."

"Wow, I know John would have liked this." Sophia said wistfully.

"Sophie, John died a hero's death. He probably should never have gone on that mission, but He did something He believed in. It's been a year now that He has been gone, we can discuss this later, ok? Right now, I want you to enjoy yourself little sister," Jennie chided her giving her a quick hug.

"Ok, ok, look at that!" Sophia pointed over to an ironworker making shields.

"Let's go watch him," Jennie pulled Sophia by the arm and drug her over to watch the armor being made.

Sophia looked around and saw Lamorak and Richard checking out a horse. Lamorak looked her way and smiled. She smiled and waved back then turned to watch the amazing transformation before her of metal being made into beautiful shields and knightly armor.

"Jennie, look there's a fiddler. Let's go listen to him play." Sophia told her sister as she turned to run over to the musician. He was really good, Sophia closed her eyes and listened. Sophia was a professional violinist.

She grew up playing, even learning how to build violins with her Grandfather as her teacher. She had such a love of them, Sophia could never resist violin music.

"Sophie when he's done, ask him if you can play something," Jennie urged her.

Sophia opened her eyes and looked at Jennie in horror.

"Me play the violin in King Arthur's Court?"

"Yes, Cundrie is probably already in our world and can't tell anyone about you anyway. There is nothing to lose, so have a little fun." She said nudging Sophia.

The musician finished and to Sophia's embarrassment Jennie spoke up!

"That was lovely, do you think you could let my sister play something with your violin?" Jennie asked him.

"Sure, I could use a break," he handed Sophia his violin and walked away to get something to drink before she could refuse.

"What should I play?" Sophia asked Jennie.

"I don't know, do that thing you do," She told her.

Sophia just smiled and shook her head, then started playing. She really got into it and closed her eyes as the music touched her very soul. When she looked up after the piece she played there was a huge crowd around her. They yelled, "Play more, play more!"

Sophia started another song and the owner of the violin sat down next to her picking up some Small Pipes he had laying there and started playing along. They must have played for an hour. The crowd was enjoying the entertainment; Sophia was getting thirsty but kept playing. The crowd had become so large that people drug over seats for the ones in front so the people in the back could see and listen.

Lamorak finally passed Sophia a drink of water to her great relief; She profoundly thanked him.

"Are we running late for the King?" She whispered to him.

"No, because he has the seat of honor listening." He pointed up to a balcony and King Arthur waved at them. They waved back and then Sophia turned to the bagpiper and said, "Do you know any marches?"

"Yes, I do, you start one and I'll follow."

So, they played until it got dark. Sophia finally handed the violin back to him thanking him for the great fun and use of his violin.

"You are welcome my Lady, let's play together again soon," He said taking a bow.

"I would enjoy that, thank you so much" Sophia said standing up as he kissed her hand.

After that Lamorak took her arm and led over to her sister and Richard, as they walked away towards the castle. Lamorak just kept smiling at Sophia, she was full of surprises.

"That was beautiful I could listen to you play all day."

"Thank you, I could play all day." She told him.

"That was incredible Sophie, I told you it would be ok." Jennie said.

"I know, thank you big sister," Sophia gave her a hug. She really meant it. She was happy for the first time in a year.

"Let's head into dinner." Lamorak said as they followed behind him into the dinner hall.

A servant met them.

"King Arthur would be honored to have you as his guests tonight, please follow me." He said.

They were placed next to King Arthur, Sophia was on one side of him with Lamorak; her sister and Richard were on the other side of him. That way they could all talk.

"It's an honor to eat with you sir," Sophia told him.

"Please call me Arthur," He said.

Then when dinner was served He got straight to the point.

"I believe, my half-sister Morgan Le Fay and your sister –in- law Cundrie, took my wife and went somewhere. I'm asking for your help. Supposedly there is some interest in where you have come from Sophia, and it has something to do with their disappearances. Either my wife left willingly or was taken." Then King Arthur waited for one of us to answer.

"I believe Cundrie has interest in Sophia's history and that She has talked to your sister, Morgan. Then the two of them convinced Guinevere to go with them on an adventure." Lamorak stated.

The King was amazed but didn't let on.

"Jennie and I need to make a trip home soon, we can look for them." Sophia told him.

"That would be good, I've spoken with Merlin and he told me to do nothing at this point in time." The King said.

"I think that's a good plan," answered Richard.

"Me too, could you please excuse me for a moment?" Sophia said standing up, "I need to use the ladies room, I will be right back. Can you point me in the right direction?" She asked.

"I'll join you," said Jennie standing up.

"Yes, go out the way you came in then go down the hall outside the dining room. It's on the right." Said Arthur.

"Ok we'll be right back."

"Do you want me to escort you?" Asked Lamorak.

"No but thank you. Jennie and I can manage ourselves." Sophia told him smiling.

They walked out of the dining room and down the hall. Before Sophia knew what happened, she was grabbed from behind!

7

SOPHIA SCREAMED, but the hand over her mouth stopped her from making a noise. Jennie turned around and they knocked her out. Leaving her on the ground. Sophia was drug out of the Castle into the stable then roughly thrown into a carriage. The carriage took off out of the courtyard; over the moat and down the hill out of Camelot leaving a trail of dust it its wake.

"What do you want?" Sophia asked.

"We have your device and are trying to find the hole but can't. You're going to show us. There's a man on the other end and we want to meet him." Answered Morgan Le Fay.

"What do you plan on doing on the other side?" Sophia asked.

"Learning something to change history." she snorted.

Finally, they got to the area and Sophia was drug out of the carriage. She wasn't shocked, but there stood Cundrie, and Iago the page he was holding on to Guinevere, who as blindfolded and tied up. Sophia was shoved from behind and pushed towards the rock. All of a sudden Sophia saw the opening and showed them. They shoved Sophia to the ground. She hit her head and passed out. Then Cundrie, Iago, and Guinevere all went through. When Sophie woke up Lamorak was holding her hand, Jennie was wiping the dirt off of the bump on her head. Kanani was licking her face. See, you need to stop leaving me behind. I would have protected you!

"I'm so glad you found me," I mumbled then passed out again.

When I woke up, it was morning. I was in my cot at Camelot and everyone was standing around me. I tried to sit up. Jennie saw me struggling and ran over to help me. I had a king-sized headache. Kanani was sitting beside me with a paw draped over my chest.

"Here drink something sweetie." Jennie said bending over.

I had a drink of water then felt really hungry, but first I had to let them know what happened.

"We must let the King know that Guinevere did not leave on her own. She was tied up and blindfolded. They said some man was going to meet them. I bet that was Grandpa, he will take care of those nasty women and Guinevere will be ok. We need to go back soon though." I finished my speech and Lamorak came over and held my hand.

"Let's get you and Jennie ready to travel. How's your head?"

"It's sore, but I'll survive. We need to get home." She told him.

They spent that day getting things in order; Sophia was feeling better by the end of the day. The next morning very early before the Knight's meeting at the Round Table, Richard and Lamorak took them to the rock.

Richard and Jennie kissed then said goodbye. "I won't be gone long, and I'll be back with our daughter. So decide where we want to build our house, we have a lot of money in a bank in

Switzerland. The money may not be worth anything here but we can buy stuff in our time and bring it through the portal for building our house here."

"Ok dear, be careful and come back soon." Richard replied.

With that she walked over and shook Lamorak's hand.

"Take good care of each other while were gone." She said.

"I will Lady Jennie," he said with tears in his eyes.

He turned to Sophia and kissed her hand. "I pray I see you again Lady Sophia. I have never met anyone like you."

"Thank you Lamorak, I will try to come back someday. I have never met anyone like you either. Thank you for everything you've done for me. I will miss you." She said giving him one last and an affectionate kiss on his right cheek.

Then she turned around, grabbed Jennie's hand, called Kanani, and stepped through time.

8

THEY WERE on the other side in a flash and Jennie followed Sophia out of the cave. There stood Susan, Leila and Kimo!

"I can't believe it!" Screamed Susan grabbing me, hugging me so tight I thought she was going to suffocate me.

Leila jumped into her mother's arms. We all hugged, talked at once then exhausted decided to go home.

"Oh, Susan did you see anyone else come through time on your watch?" Sophia asked.

"No, Sophie, just the three of you." She was counting Kanani too.

"Oh, ok I was just wondering. I need to ask Grandpa if he knows anything."

Susan was so happy to see Sophia and Kanani. Jennie was so delighted to see Leila that the conversation died on that subject.

When they arrived home, Jennie toured the house while Sophia excused herself and soaked for a longtime in her Jacuzzi bathtub; it felt therapeutic as it relaxed her muscles and allowed her mind to drift into a la-la land.

She joined everyone for dinner before sunset feeling much more comfortable. They talked through the night taking time out to call Grandpa and planned on a trip to see him the next day. He assured everyone that Guinevere and Morgan were with him and presented no problems. Iago more or less latched onto Cundrie as soon as they got to the monastery. Neither one of them had been heard from or seen since. Sophia worried about that! Grandpa was a bit concerned as well wondering what they might be doing and are they about to interfere with the flow of time and events of the past by taking back future knowledge.

Grandpa was wondering what they might be doing and are they about to interfere with the flow of time and events of the past by taking back future knowledge.

Grandpa knew even a minor change of events in the past could have a ripple effect through time drastically effecting and changing the present.

The next morning, they arrived at the Monastery right on time and Grandpa was waiting for them in the courtyard.

"Hi Grandpa," Sophia said hugging him. She couldn't believe she was back in her world.

"Hi sweetie, I'm so happy to see you safe and sound." He said. "Hi everyone, Jennie come here my love." They had a long hug too.

"Hi Kanani," Grandpa gave her a hug too.

Kanani wagged her tail. Nice see you again too.

"You're a good girl for looking after Sophie." He said scratching Kanani's head.

Kanani wagged her tail. Sophie and I are best friends, nothing will happen to her with me around. Said Kanani in a confident manner.

After a little while we were drinking herbal tea and sitting around a large circular wooden table in the Monastery. It looked and felt a little like a particular round table in the other world.

"Well, you've stirred up quite a bit of trouble in the Middle Ages Sophie," Grandpa said looking at Sophia.

"I guess so, how it is going with them?" She asked.

"We convinced Guinevere to stay a while and learn some humility before returning. She is already believing she wants Lancelot to leave the Castle, she was horrified to find out she was the one to destroy Camelot. So, they will return home soon, perhaps a bit wiser and better and hopefully be very cautious how they go about altering even minor events so as not to change the outcome of future history."

Grandpa finished. "However, last night as you slept, we located and now have knowledge of Cundrie and Iago's whereabouts. I will keep my eyes open if I hear of any trouble and let you know."

"Fantastic, I guess it's ok to mess with history if it saves lives as long as you're careful."

"We have some things to do for Jennie and Leila's return. We'll stop in to see you before they go back Grandpa." Sophia told him. With that they said goodbye.

"Ok, see you soon my dears." Grandpa saw them off.

They arrived home after doing some errands and spent the evening talking about their visit with Grandpa.

The next morning Sophia got up early or so she thought, but Susan had a spread of food out for everyone already prepared.

"Wow, Susan this is really thoughtful of you! Thank you," Sophie said, and then gave Susan a morning hug.

"You're welcome, we have a schedule to keep today, let's get everyone up and eat so we can get going."

She then passed the plates of food around when everyone was sitting down around the table.

Kanani had already been let out and was in the kitchen eating her breakfast too.

They finished, and Sophia said, "I need to shower then I'll be ready to leave. With that she got up and went into her room with Kanani close behind. They reappeared thirty-five minutes later.

Sophia was wearing a black jean skirt, blouse and Keen sandals. "Oh, it feels good to be in my own clothes again, how I missed my skirt and shoes."

Sophia had a decision to make. Did she want to stay or go back in time? It was hard to leave the luxuries of this world, but she and Kanani would have such a good time in the other world. Perhaps even make a favorable difference in history. She really had to search her soul about any decisions she was going to make.

~~~~~~

A month went by and Sophia still had not told Jennie what she had decided, so one morning Jennie approached her.

~~~~~~

"Little sister we need to get some money out of the bank. I need to go back, Richard is by now wondering where we are and Leila needs to get settled in her new environment."

"Yes, I agree with you. I have prayed about it and thought long and hard, I've made a decision; Jennie follow me please." She called everyone around the kitchen table.

"This has not been an easy decision, but Kanani and I are going back through time with Jennie and Leila. There is no reason for me to remain here unless anyone can think of something. Susan what do you and Kimo want to do?" Sophia asked.

"Great Sophie. We were waiting for you to make a decision. We're going where you go.

We can lockup the house here and come back from time to time." Kimo told her.

"Ok," Sophia shouted getting excited. "I need teaching supplies, we need to go to the bank and we need to go shopping!"

Sophia jumped up and grabbed her purse. Kanani went bounding over to her and Sophie snapped on her leash, grabbing the motorhome keys on the way out of the door. Everyone hurried out after her.

They piled in; their first stop was the bank. Then they bought schoolbooks, pencils and paper.

"What do you want to take with you Leila?" Sophie asked her niece.

"Lots and lots of paper and colored pencils." She shouted jumping up and down.

"Ok, off to the art supply store!"

They went to the fabric store and bought yards and yards of material. They bought anything that looked like it was from the Middle Ages.

Finally, they arrived home; it took them many trips to unload the motorhome.

They packed things in wheeled crates, so they could drag them behind themselves. Susan and Jennie ran into the sewing room and started making clothes.

Sophie grabbed Kanani's leash. "Come girl, let's go see Grandpa. Leila do you want to come with us?"

"Yes, let me tell Mom." Leila answered.

They went to see Grandpa and give him the news. He gave them two phones, so they would be able to keep in touch with him. He said that his guests would be going back in a month from now. He said he just might accompany them and go for the visit. Leila and Sophie were thrilled!

"I will always be in touch with you," Sophie told him.

"I know you will, go and live an exciting happy life Sophie. Teach those youngsters well. Leila you grow into a nice young lady, I am so proud of you. I love you all. When are you going? I want to be there to say goodbye."

"We are leaving Saturday, Grandpa can you drive us there?" Sophie asked.

"Yes, I wouldn't miss it for the world honey. I'll be there by eight a.m., is that ok?" he asked.

"Yes, that's perfect, thank you Grandpa!"

"Thank you for asking me." He got up and gave Sophie a big hug.

He laughed, "You girls get home and pack."

With that he walked them out to the car. Sophie could only wonder about his houseguests. She really doubted any of them except Guinevere would be reformed.

That night, the next day, and evening they packed.

"Sophia, are you taking your Stradivarius?" Asked Jennie.

"Yes, I am taking the Stradivarius. Why should it sit in a safe by itself when I love playing it? I could donate it to a museum, but I love playing it and it's mine." Sophia had talked herself into it.

"Ok, then let's get it packed. You might as well take the Juzek too, right?" Jennie asked her.

"Yes, absolutely!" She said going into the walk-in safe and grabbing her two violins.

Susan came in with Kimo, bringing in prepared boxes for the violins. They knew she wouldn't leave them. She assisted Kimo in getting them placed securely. He taped down the top and sides of the heavily padded box. The violins were packed for a safe journey. Jennie had left to go help Leila pack her last-minute things. Sophia didn't know how she was going to sleep that night with all of the anticipation of going back in time again. She could hardly believe it happened the first time!

9

SOPHIA WAS right; she could hardly sleep that night. She got up two times and walked through the motorhome, going over the checklists. Finally, at midnight she was so exhausted, she joined Kanani who was already in bed. Kanani put her paw around Sophie's neck and that is how they slept until Grandpa woke them up the next morning.

Grandpa arrived at six a.m., not 8 a.m. like he was supposed to.

"Good morning Papa," Sophie said opening the door and giving him a kiss. "Come in and I'll put on some coffee."

"Good morning sweetheart! Sorry I'm so early, I couldn't sleep with the fear of over sleeping and not making it here in time to take you."

"It's ok," Sophie said as she trailed off into the kitchen putting on the pot of coffee.

"Make yourself at home Grandpa, I have to go get dressed and get the others up.

"Ok, sweetheart," Grandpa said take your time. Then he sat down at the kitchen table spreading out his newspaper to read it.

At least they were all packed, Sophia thought as she went to knock on bedroom doors.

"Grandpa's here, everyone up," She shouted as She passed the bedroom doors knocking on them on the way to her own room.

Pretty soon everyone was dressed, including Sophia and they had coffee. Susan grabbed the sweet rolls and placed them out for everyone. It's just what they needed for a quick sugar high before their journey through time.

They finished, cleaned up and walked out of the house. Kimo locked the door; Sophia followed him into the motor-home. She looked back and had no regrets. She had made her decision. Finally, they were at the caves. Sophia had butterflies in her stomach and she was sure everyone else did too. Sophie was sure Kanani was the only one without a care. They got out of the motorhome and Grandpa brought out a box of phones! Well he wanted to make sure they would always stay in touch with him.

Sophia turned towards him and said, "Ok goodbye for now Grandpa, you promised to come see us soon." Sophia gave him a big hug and goodbye kiss.

"Yes, I will, goodbye for now Sophie. I will miss you, but you have enough phones to stay in touch. I'll come soon to see all of you. Perhaps after you build your homes." Grandpa hugged everyone goodbye.

"Jennie, you go first then we will send in the crates. After that Leila can go, then Kanani and myself. Kimo I think it best you come in at the end. Does that sound good to all of you?" Sophia asked.

"Yes, it's perfect," answered Jennie. Everyone agreed.

Jennie stepped through then they started sending their belongings.

It was Leila's turn, "Ok Leila go through sweetie." Sophie told her.

"I'm so excited, bye Grandpa," She said as she stepped through. She didn't hear his response.

"Kanani come here girl," Sophie grabbed her leash and they stepped through together." Sophie turned before disappearing and saw Grandpa waving goodbye, he had tears in his eyes.

Kanani and Sophie repeated their landing experience. Kanani jumped on Sophie and knocked her down again. Then she started jumping back and forth over her.

I'm so happy to be here with you, Kanani was saying in doggie talk.

Sophia looked up and was shocked to see Lamorak standing there laughing at them.

Kanani saw Lamorak and ran over to greet him too.

Richard was already arranging their belongings with Leila and Jennie.

"What were you two doing here?" Sophie asked with complete dismay.

"We have been here every day waiting for Jennie and Leila. I only had faith that I'd ever see you again." Lamorak answered.

Just then Kimo and Susan landed behind Sophie. She turned with a smile on her face and said, "Welcome my dear friends."

"Let me introduce you to Lamorak and Jennie's husband Richard."

"Nice to meet you," Lamorak said shaking Kimo's hand and bending to kiss Susan's.

"Nice to meet you too," Kimo said.

"So nice to meet such a gentleman," said Susan.

Sophie looked at Lamorak and they both laughed. Richard walked over and introduced himself too.

"Let's walk over to that pub," Lamorak said pointing across the road. "Then I can send someone to Camelot and get two carriages for everything."

"What a lovely idea," Susan said grabbing Sophie by the hand. "A real English pub! I'm so excited, come on Kimo let's go."

They walked in and sat at a long table. They ordered drinks and had a good English lunch of bread, cheese and meat. Lamorak joined them shortly after sending finding a runner to take his message to Camelot.

"It will be at two hours for the transportation, let us enjoy our time and catch up."

"Thank you Lamorak, great idea!" Sophie said adding,

"Guinevere and Morgan will be back over in about a month or so. Grandpa said they are enjoying their stay and will be changed people when they come back." She added.

"Really? It will be something to see Morgan changed! How about Cundrie and Iago?" He laughed taking a bite of bread.

"They disappeared!" Sophie exclaimed.

"Well I am sure they will stir up some trouble, I hope they are found by your Grandfather soon!" Lamorak exclaimed.

"Me too!" She replied.

"Wouldn't it be lovely to save Camelot and change history!" exclaimed Leila.

"Would it be right to change history?" Susan asked Lamorak.

"For the better it would," Lamorak answered.

"I agree," said Jennie. Everyone else just nodded thoughtfully.

An hour and a half later Leila saw the carriages approaching.

"Look they're here," Leila said running to the window.

"So, they are, that didn't take long did it Lamorak?" Sophie asked him.

"No, it didn't," he answered. "Ok everyone let me pay the tab and then let's go out and load up. Ladies use the boot if you have too, it's a long dirty trip." Then he got up to pay our bill.

"Ok, Lamorak we'll be right back," Sophie told him.

She walked to the restroom Jennie and Susan.

Jennie said, "We can't let him pay for everything, Sophie we have a lot of money."

"I know but we need to exchange it somehow. I won't let him pay for everything, I promise." She said giving her a hug.

"Ok," Jennie was satisfied.

By the time they met the men and Leila outside, the bags were loaded in one carriage. Leila had convinced the driver of the other carriage to let her sit in front with him. Jennie, Susan, Kanani and I rode inside. Kimo got on the carriage with our luggage, sitting with the driver. Not that anyone needed help, but it seemed an ok thing to do.

It happened about an hour into the trip. They were under attack by bandits! Bows and arrows started shooting at them.

10

"DUCK LEILA!" Sophie shouted out the window. "Give me your hand! Sophie put her arm out as far as she could.

Leila turned towards Sophie, but a bandit grabbed her before Sophie could get a hold of her hand. He carried her off kicking and screaming! Their driver was killed and fell beneath the wheels. Jennie was leaning out of the carriage screaming at the bandit riding off with Leila. Richard took off after him. Sophie climbed out the window and started going towards the front of the carriage. As she did this she glanced away to see Lamorak kill one bandit with a swift swipe of his sword and start chasing another. Just then her dress snagged on a low bush something as she exited out the window.

"Careful, Sophie," Susan cried getting up to help her. She lost her balance and fell from the run-away carriage. Susan was screaming at her too, as she looked out of the window Sophie had just fallen out of.

Kanani was barking, Sophie, I'm here! Don't worry I'll come for you.

Kimo's driver was wounded, but Kimo was able to stop their carriage. Lamorak saw what happened and caught up to the run-away carriage grabbing the frightened horses by their reins and bringing it to a controlled stop. Kanani jumped out the window and ran over to Sophie. She was still lying in the dirt totally shaken trying to sit up and unsnag her dress.

"Sophie," yelled Lamorak jumping off of his horse and running over to her, "are you hurt?"

"I'm just sore and my dress is ripped," she told him as he knelt beside her.

"Can you stand up?" he asked to take her hand.

"Yes, thank you." she said.

Susan and Jennie jumped out of the carriage and ran towards her too. Kanani beat them though and she was licking Sophie's face.

"Thank you, girl," Sophia said trying to get her to stop.

I told you I would save you, Kanani was saying in doggie licks.

"Where's Richard?" Sophia asked, finally succeeding in pushing her off.

"He chased the rider that grabbed Leila!" Shouted Jennie as she came up checking me out to make sure Sophia was ok.

"Here he comes now!" Jennie cried turning to run towards her husband. "Where is she?" Jennie cried.

"I almost had them and got ambushed by others hiding amongst the trees. I lost her Jennie! He cried out, h was so upset.

"What do we do?" Jennie asked Lamorak, "Do you know who they were? Where they might have gone?"

"Yes, I do, we need to get to Camelot as soon as possible, get some knights and go get hr." He said as he was helping Sophia over to the carriage.

Kimo was holding both carriages in place. "Kimo can you drive the carriage with the luggage?" Asked Lamorak.

"Yes, Lamorak I can," He said, "I think I have the hang of it."

"Good, Richard if you could grab my horse I'll drive the women."

"Ok," said Richard going over and getting Lamorak's horse.

"Everyone get in please," Lamorak was helping Sophia get seated. Kanani was sitting on Sophia's feet inside the carriage. Lamorak climbed up front and they started off.

With Kimo being a novice carriage driver, and with the wounded driver and the grief-stricken Richard, leading

Lamorak's horse, they didn't move as fast as they could have.

They slowly limped into Camelot. Yglais came running out of her tent.

"Mother, get Perceval and Accalon to come here. We were attacked by the Dark Bandits, they killed Ivan and took Jennie's little girl!"

Yglais put her hands over her mouth in horror, "No, this is dreadful!" She cried as she turned and did what her son had asked of her.

Lamorak got Sophia out and into a comfortable sitting position. Women came and attended to the wounded driver.

Accalon and Perceval arrived with ten knights ready to go.

"Thank you, Mother, Men we need a plan!" Lamorak commanded.

"I want to go too," said Kimo.

"No, you are needed here Kimo. You can arrange for more tents to be put up and I need you to take care of the women." Lamorak told him, relief flooded through Susan who objected that he goes.

"Ok, I agree I can't leave my women, can I?" Where do I get more tents?"

"My mother knows, and she will assist you." Lamorak told him.

"Time is being wasted, let's ride!" Lamorak shouted. He would formulate a plan as they rode.

The knights cheered, and Sophia cringed.

11

"BE CAREFUL and come back alive," Sophia pleaded.

"We will My Lady, don't worry. We have the greatest knights around. Will you be ok?" he asked.

"Yes, just hurry back," she told him.

"Ok goodbye then!" Lamorak called as he charged off in front of the knights.

"Sophie I'm so scared," said Jennie grabbing her hand.

"Me too," Sophia cried. "This is tragic."

"Sophie and Jennie, I'm going to help Kimo get the tents set up, then I will come back and help around here."

"Thank you, Susan," Sophia told her. As Susan left to help Kimo Yglais approached Sophia.

"Let's look at you my dear," Yglais said. "Let's get you out of these filthy clothes and see what damage has been done. You're going to be very sore later on, I just want to make sure nothing is broken."

"Thank you, Jennie can you come with us?" Sophia asked her sister.

"Yes, sweetie let's go," Jennie said.

Then they took her into the tent and Sophia got cleaned up. She had a very bruised leg and back with some scratches, but nothing seemed to be broken.

Kanani was right behind Sophia. I'm here with you. Look I can make you feel better. Kanani was rubbing up against Sophia whining.

"Kanani I don't mean to ignore you. Of course, you can come with us girl." Sophia seemed to read her dog's mind.

12

LAMORAK LED the knights deep into the forest, and then suddenly put up his hand for complete stillness and quiet. They heard horses riding through the forest. "Get your arrows ready," he whispered.

He positioned everyone off the main path on two sides. Just within the trees. They came closer and closer; he put down his arm to signal the attack. The battle was bloody; many of the Dark Bandits were killed.

"Where is the child?" Lamorak commanded talking to a fallen Bandit with his sword pointed at his chest. "I will spare your life if you tell me where she is!"

"The child is tied up a mile from here in a tree," he spat out.

"Show me!" Commanded Lamorak as he roughly jerked the captive to his feet.

Lamorak followed the man while leading his horse. Richard and a few knights fell behind Lamorak while the others were waiting for their return on the main road.

"Daddy!" Screamed Leila when she saw them coming. "I'm up here."

"I see you baby, were coming." Richard shouted back hurrying as fast as he could.

They got there, and Richard climbed the rope ladder to cut her loose.

"Oh Daddy," she sobbed, "I was so scared!"

"I know honey, but you're alright now." He hugged his daughter and brought her down, then placed her in front of him on his saddle.

Lamorak pushed the bandit and told him to go away. He could have killed him, and any other man would have, but to Lamorak that seemed immoral and he wasn't going to lose his soul.

With that they caught up with the other knights and returned to Camelot.

13

KIMO HAD more tents set up, while Susan made the beds, then put away their clothes. Most their luggage was put away, except for the school supplies by the time the knights came back to camp. Richard rode into camp with Leila; Jennie ran over and grabbed her off the saddle. She hugged her so tight it hurt, but Leila didn't care. She was home with her family again.

Sophia was starting to be in terrible pain from her fall off the carriage. She wished she had a painkiller; Lamorak came over to see how she was doing. Sophia asked him to help her into her tent to lie down.

"Can you come back for me in an hour?" she asked him.

"Yes, do you want me to stay?"

"No, I need to try and get ahold of my Grandpa but thank you for asking."

"You are welcome, I'll check back soon." he said, then turned around and left.

Sophia reached into her pack and got out her phone. She turned it on while Kanani jumped up on her bed waiting to snuggle.

I'm here with you Sophie, I love you.

"Are you ok girl?" Sophia asked her, Kanani wagged her tail and Sophia rubbed her head. It was such a comfort to have her. Picking up the phone se dialed Grandpa's number. He answered on the first ring.

"Hi Sophie, you made it my dear! I am so pleased to hear from you." Grandpa wouldn't let Sophia get a word in.

Finally, she got to speak. "Grandpa we made it, but there was an incident soon after we returned; then she relayed the story."

"Well I'm glad Leila was unhurt, but what about you dear, do you need to come home and get checked out at the hospital?" he sounded concerned.

"I think I will be ok Grandpa, I will go back if I need too, but it will just take time for these bruises to heal. At least I didn't hit my head, so I know I will be fine." she reassured him. The hour went by quickly, because Lamorak came into Sophia's tent before she was done talking to Grandpa on the phone.

"I will call you tomorrow Grandpa, I have to go. I love you," she told him.

"Goodbye dear, I love you too." With that they disconnected.

"I brought you some dinner, then why don't you try to rest Sophia. We can get more done tomorrow if you aren't so sore and tired." He handed her a plate of food and set a dish down for Kanani too.

Oh, thank you Lamorak, you are a pretty good host, Kanani was thinking as she gobbled her dinner.

"Thank you, I'm forever grateful," Sophia was saying as she took the dish of food from him. He sat down next to her and they talked until she finished. Then he took Kanani out for potty.

When he came back with her they said good night. Sophia got up and brushed her teeth then went to bed, with Kanani sleeping next to her.

Well as long as I'm with you Sophie I don't care if we don't have our comfy bed back home. Kanani was thinking as she fell asleep.

Sophia dreamed of bandits and of John. Could she go back in time and find him before he gets killed? Was that possible? Should she just let it go and pursue saving Lamorak and educating children in this century? Tomorrow would bring new adventures.

14

A FEW MONTHS had gone by, Sophia's bruises were healed and the builders they had hired were hard at work building their homes. They decided to build them in Camelot, because Sophia wanted to open a school closer to where more children lived. Also, it was much safer being in Camelot than where Lamorak's castle was located. King Arthur sent out several knights on a quest, one that Lamorak was supposed to be on, but didn't go because of Sophia. It was a good thing, because those knights were ambushed and brutally killed. They were on a quest to save the last of the white dragons. Rival knights from the north, looking to kill the dragons, ambushed and killed all of the King's knights that went on the mission.

It was late one afternoon that Sophia noticed again how Kanani kept disappearing at the same time of day. This was a dog that would never leave her side. Today, Sophia excused herself from her sister when she saw Kanani taking off again. They were watching over the builders, getting minor details fixed.

Too Sophia's amazement she saw Merlin the Wizard! Should she be worried? That sneaky little dog, what was she up to without me?

Sophia followed them through the market; people threw Kanani tidbits of food. Sophia was getting upset; she didn't like Kanani to go off of her diet like that. She had to change things soon.

Next, they went through the cemetery gate by the side of the castle. She followed them through and watched them go around to the back of the castle and go through a door. Merlin unlocked it and let Kanani in, then himself.

What was this about? Should se wait? She decided to hide behind a headstone and see what would happen next. Sophia made herself as comfortable as possible. It was getting later in the afternoon and her stomach was growling, she was hungry. It was time to go back and make dinner, but she decided to wait ten more minutes. Finally, he door opened and Kanani came out running right past Sophia, high tailing it back home without noticing her.

Pant pant, I'd better hurry, Sophia will be looking for me. Kanani sprinted through the market not even stopping to beg.

Merlin left shortly after and presumably went back to his place. Sophia hesitantly went over to the door and turned the knob. It was a heavy door, Merlin forgot to lock it, she pulled it open. Sophia walked into the dark cold hall, she couldn't see in front of her so she put her hand against the wall. She felt her way down the winding hallway and then all of a sudden someone spoke to her! She stifled a scream and held her breath. She wanted to run!

15

"WHO GOES there?" The voice said.

Sophia froze, terrified.

"I know you're there, say something!" The voice said again getting agitated.

"Um, Sophie."

"Well, who is Sophie?" The voice asked.

"Kanani's human," she answered shakily.

"Oh, I like Kanani. Do you know Merlin?" The voice continued the conversation. It sounded like a young voice.

"Yes, not well but I saw him. I noticed Kanani missing every day for a while and today followed her to see what she was up too. Who are you," Sophia asked?

"My name is Gunther, I'm a friendly dragon." he replied.

"A DRAGON?" Sophia shouted! She didn't mean to shout, but a dragon? She didn't believe in dragons.

"I won't hurt you!" he whined back at her.

Sophia grabbed the wall tighter and inched forward two more steps. She peaked around the corner. She was amazed; it was the most beautiful place she had ever seen. It must have been the length of the whole castle! There were lights, windows, trees, grass, and a cave for Gunther. There was everything here to make him feel like he was living outside. Then she laid her eyes on Gunther! He was the most beautiful creature she had ever-laid eyes on!

"What are you doing in King Arthur's dungeon?" she asked him.

He answered saying, "Men are killing all of the white dragons. There was an awful battle, my parents were killed and King Arthur saved me. I was a baby and he brought me here to hide me. There are more of us that need saving. Merlin comes to talk to me and feed me daily. I dream of being outside and being able to go wherever I want to go. Merlin agrees something must be done with me soon."

"Well, let me see what I can find out. Is there anything I can bring you? "

"Yes, will you come back again with Kanani to talk to me?" Asked the dragon.

"Yes, but I must go for now, I will be back tomorrow."

"Ok, good night," Gunther told her.

"Good night, Gunther," she told him, then turned around and made her way back down the hallway and outside. She closed the door and sat down in disbelieving awe. Sophia looked around. Did she just talk to a dragon? She had to go find Lamorak.

16

SOPHIA RAN back to their homes being built, found Kanani and stared at her. She jumped on Sophia and gave her tons of kisses.

"I know what you've been doing," Sophia told her.

All Sophia heard was woof, but Kanani was really saying. What do you mean? I'm a good girl. She cocked her head looking at Sophia like a little innocent dog.

"Hmm, let's get my sister if she's still here, go back to camp and start dinner. I need to find Lamorak," Sophia told her.

She looked around; Jennie had already gone back to camp so Kanani and Sophie decided to see what had been done that day. The homes were almost complete. She was getting so excited!

They got back to the camp and everyone wanted to know where they had been. So, sitting around the table at dinner that evening she confided in her sister, Leila, Richard, Susan, Kimo, and Lamorak, who had made it back from working with King Arthur that day.

"Did you know anything about this Lamorak?" she asked him

Yes, I knew King Arthur had saved a dragon, but never had a clue he was in the bottom part of the castle! It doesn't seem like a good place to live for a dragon, does it?" He asked looking at her with a questionable expression.

"No, it doesn't, and he said that there were more that needed saving, which we know already." she replied quickly.

"Yes, well I will speak to Merlin tomorrow. Are you and Kanani up for a quest, Sophie?" He asked her.

She looked at him with shock, "What kind of quest?" she asked him with suspicion. "The kind where we take Gunther and go find his relatives, then bring them back here. There are caves back behind where you're building your homes. We could make a nice place for them back there and then they could help keep a watch over Camelot!" he exclaimed.

"Well, that's a grand plan, let me think about it tonight and let's see what Merlin has cooked up before we decide, ok?" she answered.

"Ok, sounds logical," he said.

"I want to go too!" Piped in Leila.

"Oh no you won't do that!" Said Jennie to her daughter.

"Mommmm, pleassssseeeee?" Pleaded Leila.

Before Jennie could answer Sophie said, "Leila, let's see what the plans are and not worry about it tonight, deal?"

"Ok, but you had better not leave me behind," she grumbled.

Susan just laughed as she got up to clean the dishes.

Sophia got up, gave Leila a hug and helped Susan; then they joined the others by the campfire singing their evening away.

The next morning, Jennie, Leila, Susan, Kimo and Yglais left to go check on the progress of the builders. Richard, Lamorak and Sophia met with Merlin in his house. Then they had a meeting with King Arthur and it was decided that a quest was to begin. They would leave as soon as they could get everything together. Sir Lamorak, Sir Perceval, Sir Accalon, Sir Degore, Sir Alymere, Sir Bedivere, Sir Lancelot, Merlin, Kanani, and Sophia would be in the party. Gunther was consulted, and he was getting very excited about being with them. They drew up a plan that if they were attacked, Kanani and Sophia were to get on Gunther and he would take them to safety.

At dinner that night Sophia was so thrilled she could hardly eat. Lamorak and Sophia had filled the others in on their meetings that day. Leila wanted to go so badly, but her mother and Sophie told her it was far too dangerous, and she needed to remain at home. Sophie assured her that she would have plenty of dragons to play with if they were successful. That satisfied her somewhat. Sophie was worried about taking Kanani, but there was no way she would stay here without her. She knew she would try and find her and that would be far more dangerous for her. Sophia debated on taking one of her violins; she had never been without one since the age of four. It would be a shame for her to lose the Stradivarius and she loved her Juzek just as much. So, she decided perhaps this would be the first time she would be without a violin.

Yes, I am leaving it here, she told herself.

The morning of their departure saw all of Camelot out cheering or their success. They were on a quest to rescue the remaining white dragons in the world! They would be up against other kingdoms if any rivaling knights crossed their path. They would be traveling far far away to a distant land. They would have Merlin report to King Arthur on their progress. No one knew how long they would be gone.

Gunther was having so much fun; he practiced flying every day to get ready for this quest, so he was in fine form by the time they departed.

Kanani was placed on a horse with Sophie; all of the knights were ahead of them. I'm so excited! Sophie always does such fun things! Gunther and Merlin were riding beside them. Jennie was crying, and then ran over trying to stop Sophia by waving her hands.

Sophia stopped her horse and when Jennie reached her she said, "Don't forget your phone so you can call when the quest is finished Sophie," and then she handed Sophie the phone.

"Thank you, very much big sister," she said as she grabbed the phone and they continued on their way.

Sophia saw Susan running over to Jennie putting her arm around her to give reassurance. Kimo was waving goodbye too. Sophie and Kanani then caught up with Merlin.

They traveled north all day and finally stopped to set up camp many hours later before dusk that night.

"Lamorak, how far have we come and where do you think we are?" Sophia asked him.

"We have come about 1000 paces and we have many to reach Northern Scotland. We might be in for some action with rivalry knights when we get farther north." he answered. "Here's a copy of our route in case we get separated." Sophia took the map and tucked it into her pocket.

"Thank you Lamorak."

"Gunther, do you feel good about this trip?" Sophia asked the dragon.

"Yes, I am very excited. I wish I could fly ahead and see what is there." He said.

"That would be too dangerous Gunther, that is why you must stay with us." Lamorak reminded him.

"I know," answered Gunther scratching his front paw on the ground to make a comfy bed to sleep in as the group began to settle in for the night.

They traveled two more weeks with no incidents, and then Merlin decided to let King Arthur know their whereabouts. He took out one of his doves out of his bag and tied a note on to his leg and let him go.

The next morning, they packed up and started on their way. It happened around noon when they were getting close to a forest. They walked into an ambush! Arrows flew over their heads! Sophia's horse reared up and she fell off with Kanani. Her phone slipped out of her skirt pocket. She tried to grab it, but in all the confusion missed. Lamorak jumped was off his horse grabbing her and pulling her towards Gunther. He called Gunther to come get Sophia and Kanani.

17

"GUNTHER COME here!" he yelled at the dragon.

"Hurry, take Sophia and Kanani," Lamorak told him.

Gunther put his head down and Lamorak shoved Sophia onto the big dragon, and then handed Kanani to her. Merlin jumped on too. As soon as they were on him Lamorak told him to fly away.

Then he grabbed his sword, and turned to fight. Sophia held on and looked down at the battle below. Gunther was flying fast and high so they could only see specks on the ground. She was frightened that Lamorak would get killed; that they would be lost. Merlin was sitting behind her on Gunther. That at least gave her some comfort!

I'm here with you Sophie, I love you. Slurp Slurp. Kanani kissed Sophia.

"Thank you, girl. I love you too." Sophie told her.

"I should go back and help fight," said Gunther.

"No," said Merlin, "we are here to protect you."

"Merlin, couldn't he put us somewhere and go back and fight?" Sophie pleaded.

"No, the orders were for Gunther to take off with us, Sophia. Gunther why don't you land over there." Merlin was pointing to point high small clearing deep in the forest.

Gunther turned towards the forest and slowly guided down between the trees. He let them off. Sophia looked around. It was a gorgeous jungle. However, she was visibly shaken. With a sword in her hand she sat upon a tree trunk. Kanani came over and put her head on Sophie's lap giving her comfort. Gunther put his paw beside Sophie and stared into her face. Merlin climbed a tree and looked behind them to see if anyone was coming their way. It was very peaceful. Would the others find them? Where they still alive?

18

LAMORAK WAS glad that Sophie and Kanani were safe; he went into battle with rival knight, fighting to the death. Perceval was swinging his sword and wounding his attacker. Lamorak swung his sword and killed him. Then they turned around and fought more knights coming towards them. It was a bloody battle, Lamorak was tired and his sword was growing, he looked around. The attacking knights had called a retreat and they fled taking their dead. To his sorrow, he saw that Sir Degore, Sir Alymere, and Sir Bedivere, were lying on the ground. He went over and checked, they were gone. Sir Lancelot was wounded, but able to ride, so it only left Sir Perceval, Sir Accalon, and Lamorak to bury the dead. "That was Gawain's men that attacked us, did Gawain survive?" Lamorak asked Perceval and Accalon.

"I don't know, when are they going to let this feud go? We didn't kill his father!" Yelled Perceval angrily to the fleeing rival knights.

"I don't know. Lancelot, are you ok to move forward?" asked Lamorak.

"Yes, we have some horses that didn't run off. We need to get them and ride as far as we can tonight." Lancelot answered.

With that they picked Lancelot up and mounted the horses; the doves had all flown out of the Merlin's bag and were gone. Lamorak was hoping when they all arrived in Camelot together with no message tied to them, perhaps King Arthur would know what happened and send more men to help them. They couldn't worry about that now, they needed to find Sophia and Gunther.

Where did that dragon take them? Lamorak asked himself.

19

WHEN MERLIN came down from the tree, he caught some rabbits with his magic and that is how Sophia saw him approaching. Gunther made a fire with one hot breath to keep them warm, while Sophia and Kanani gathered some herbs.

"Hi Merlin, any sign of them?" she pleaded.

"No, my dear there isn't. We can't stay out here in the open; I saw a waterfall and lake not far from here. We need to go that way, pointing towards the northwest, perhaps there will be a cave we can occupy. Let's put out this fire and start walking towards it."

"Ok, I agree, Merlin." Sophia said stomping out the fire to follow him.

A boar charged at them from the woods! Gunther killed him with his dragon fire. It was amazing; Gunther was shocked too. He had never breathed fire before! Now they had enough food for a big dinner, dragons can sure eat a lot. They drug the bore behind them and approached the waterfall. Kanani was so happy to see water she jumped in and swam around. This is so much fun!

"Look, there's a cave behind the waterfall," Merlin pointed out. "Stay here, I will see if it's empty."

"Ok," Sophia stayed where she was, watching Kanani swim. She was having a great time splashing around. Sophia laughed, in spit their situation they could still have some fun.

"The cave's empty," said Merlin, "let's make a fire at the opening."

"Oh, this is nice," Sophia said walking behind the waterfall. Kanani came running up shaking herself all over them.

Oh joy. Thanks, Kanani, just what I needed. She thought sarcastically. The opening and cave were big enough for Gunther too. They ate dinner and then sat around the fire talking about the day. Hoping that the knights were ok and coming to find them soon.

20

CASEY LANE rolled out of bed and just about hit the floor hard. The phone was ringing; it was the middle of the night and Jackie Lee, her German Shepherd Dog, had taken over her whole queen bed, covers and all. She groped for the phone.

"Casey Lane and Jackie Lee GSD Detective Agency," She mumbled into the phone.

"Yes! Yes, hello, my name is Father Anderson, I want to hire you and your dog to go find my granddaughter, she's missing. I know where she is; but it's awkward to explain over the phone. Can you fly to Luxembourg and meet me, and then I can explain?"

Casey Lane turned on the light and looked at the clock, it was five a.m. time to get up soon anyway. She was listening with interest now. Jackie Lee was snoring and lying on his back. Really, he had to get up soon too.

"Well, we can fly to Luxembourg and meet you, but I can't promise we'll accept the assignment." She told him.

"I will have tickets for you at Sea Tac, can you go tonight?"

Whew, tonight she thought!

"Umm, we just finished a big assignment, so we could catch a flight out tonight. Will you pick us up?" She asked him.

"Yes, I will be there to get you." he replied.

"Ok, let me call and make a reservation." she told him.

"It's already done; you leave at 8 P.M. tonight on Lufthansa. Have a safe flight and thank you." He replied then hung up.

Casey looked at the dead phone in her hand. What was this all about? She put the phone down thinking about all she had to do.

"Jackie Lee, up and at'em kid," she said leaning over the bed giving him morning rubs.

"Arrrr," He mumbled smiling at her with his big white teeth. Is it really morning?

"You're a character Jackie Lee, let's go." She said with a smirk.

They hit South Beach for a bit of exercise and by noon were home and packed. Casey Lane notified her boyfriend of sorts that they would be out of town, to please keep an eye on her house. He was a State Trooper, so she wasn't sure where he was right now. He wouldn't be happy she had left without saying goodbye, so that's why she at least left him a message. Jackie Lee was wearing his doggie armor suit, Casey Lane had her suitcase packed very lightly and they caught the ferry from Friday Harbor, Washington, that's where Jackie and Casey lived, to drive down to the airport in Seattle and wait for their flight.

The airline was very accommodating to Jackie Lee; he got a seat next to Casey Lane in first class. It was a bit of a fiasco getting through security with Jackie Lee's body armor.

"It was very nice of Mr. Anderson or Father Anderson to pay for our fare overseas." Casey said to Jackie Lee.

It was very nice of him. Jackie Lee thought.

Everyone one on the flight thought Jackie Lee was so adorable; of course, Casey did too.

They were greeted at the airport without a wait and driven to a beautiful estate. Father Anderson told Casey this was Sophia's house, used to be his until he joined a monastery.

They walked in; Casey Lane was stunned at the very beauty of the place. The off-white marble floors in the entryway, a huge chandelier hanging overhead, wainscoted walls, polished wooded floors, she shook her head in amazement. There seemed to be many rooms however they were shown into the kitchen.

"This is the house you and Jackie Lee can stay in tonight, I have prepared a dinner for us and thought we could talk about my proposal during that time. Then if you agree, I will take you to the destination tomorrow, does that sound good to you?" Asked Father Anderson.

"Yes, yes, could I just take Jackie Lee out for a quick walk?" Casey Lane asked him.

"Perfect idea, then I will have the food ready when you get back. What does Jackie Lee eat?" Asked Father Anderson.

"I have his food packed in dry ice, thank you for reminding me. I need to get it in the fridge right away. Then we'll go out Jackie Lee," she looked at her dog; he was giving her big eyes when she mentioned his food.

Did you say food? He got up and wagged his tail, then pawed her.

"In a minute, while I get your food unpacked, go get your leash!" She told him. With that he trotted off to the front door and came back with the leash in his mouth. He remembered she had left it at the front door as soon as they entered the house.

Everything was accomplished, Jackie Lee had his walk and dinner; he was now lying down at her feet. They were eating, and Casey Lane was listening in disbelief at the tale of Sophie and Kanani.

"Well, what do you think? Would you go and take a look, then get back to me? My older granddaughter, Jennie, is very worried about them. I think, but don't know for sure if my great granddaughter went with Sophia and Kanani as well as Lamorak and Merlin. Something must have happened, or we would have heard from them by now. They have been gone nine weeks!" He looked very worried indeed.

"I will go over and meet with Jennie, then see if I can be of any help. I don't know much about finding dragons, I don't even believe they ever really existed and I don't believe I can go back in time. However, if this is true, Jackie Lee needs to stay here with you until I return. I don't feel comfortable with him going through time. Is that a deal?" she asked.

Getting up to shake her hand Father Anderson said, "That's a deal, Jackie Lee will have to come back to the monastery with me and stay there until you return. Just tell me how to care for him and feed him. I'll be anxious to hear your report. I'll call Jennie now, so she can meet you tomorrow when you arrive." He got up and walked into another room.

Casey Lane scratched her dog on the head, "I don't believe any of this Jackie Lee, but he seems like a sane person. You be a really good boy, ok?" She didn't expect an answer, but he gave her a high five.

I'll be seeing you soon, right? Just come back for me. Man was she going to miss him.

"Ok, it's all set for tomorrow. We will leave here around seven a.m. if that's ok with you?" He asked.

"Yes, that's fine. Where should Jackie Lee and I sleep tonight? I'd like a shower too and I need to repack a smaller bag to take with me." She added.

"Follow me, you can have this guest room, there's a tub and shower attached to the room and fresh towels." He said as Casey Lane got up from the table and followed him to a room off the kitchen.

"Thank you and good night," she said as he walked away.

"Thank you too," he said turning around to look at her, "good night."

With that they were alone. She didn't know what she was getting herself into and why would anyone leave this beautiful house to go to the middle ages? Strange! She needed sleep. Pretty soon Jackie Lee was snoring away next to her. If she hadn't been so tired she would not have fallen asleep so fast herself.

Morning came all too fast, Jackie Lee was left in the car or no one could have stopped him from coming with her on her journey. She cried when they hugged goodbye.

She was talking to Father Anderson and before she knew it, she had stepped through an opening. Darkness bounded all around her, she was all alone; it went by very fast, then she landed hard on the ground. She looked around and saw a carriage coming her way.

I sure hope they're coming for me, she said to herself. Unbelievable, the old man was telling me the truth!

The carriage stopped in front of Casey Lane. Jennie jumped out of the door.

"Hi, I'm Jennie, you must be Casey Lane. Where's Jackie Lee?" Jennie stuck out her hand to shake Casey's and looked around for Jackie.

"Hi, yes I'm Casey and I left Jackie with your grandpa. I was worried about him coming through time."

"Well, Kanani has come through many times and it hasn't bothered her a bit. Kanani is a German Shepherd too. So, he would've been ok, but Grandpa will take good care of him. He loves German Shepherds. Come on, let's grab your bag and go back to Camelot." Jennie then grabbed Casey's little bag and they jumped into the carriage.

"I'm in shock. Did I really go through time?" Asked Casey.

"Yes, you did, I know it's a bit far-fetched, but it really happened. Welcome to our new world Casey. Thank you for coming. Let me catch you up on what has happened so far. By the time the carriage arrived in Camelot, Casey was up to speed on the story of Kanani, Sophia, and Gunther. She was introduced to Richard, Susan and Kimo. Then that night they sat around the campfire going over their plans. King Arthur was going with more of his knights, Richard, Jennie and yes, Leila were going too. In fact, they were taking a lot of people with them. They had their carriages loaded up the next day, Casey met King Arthur and they dressed up Jennie, Casey, and Leila in armor for women.

"You look fabulous!" Said Jennie to Casey.

"So do you!" Said Casey. "You think these will be comfortable for the long trip? I guess they want to make sure we're protected. Not exactly 'lightweight' for traveling." She laughed.

"I think they'll be fine. Wait until Richard sees how stylish I am in this armor!" Jennie laughed too.

21

YGLAIS AND AFAWEN, the maid, waved goodbye to all of them as they took off for Scotland, looking for the lost party.

There were so many of them that it looked like all of Camelot had left. Yglais was sad to see them all depart, but she prayed her sons would be found alive. Some of King Arthur's Knights had stayed behind, and Yglais was going to be busy making sure the homes were finished and the caves prepared in hopes of many dragons returning with them.

22

"ARE YOU thinking what I am Jackie Lee?" Grandpa asked Jackie Lee when they had finished a big dinner and were sitting in front of the fireplace. WOOF! Said Jackie Lee giving Grandpa a high five. I say we go get her!

"Well, I feel the same way. Let's go pack, we're going to go find them.

Grandpa jumped up and Jackie Lee took off after him. Yahoo!

He knocked on a door.

"Yes? Who is it please?"

"It's Father Anderson, can you open up Morgan Le Fay?"

The door cracked open.

"We need to talk," she opened the door and Grandpa told her what was transpiring in Camelot. She agreed they were needed back home.

"Let's go talk to Guinevere," Grandpa said as he stood up to go out of the door. The three of them went over to Guinevere's door and knocked.

"Open up, we need to talk to you about something important," Morgan sniffled as she talked.

"What's going on?" Asked Guinevere as she let them into her room.

They told her. She agreed. So, everyone departed to their own rooms and packed that evening. In the morning they were going to Camelot. The party shouldn't be too far ahead of them.

23

GUNTHER DECIDED to take a swim. He jumped into the pool of water under the waterfalls. Kanani jumped in after and swam circles around Gunther as he splashed in the water. Sophia was laughing so hard she doubled over holding her stomach. This at least was some relief from the stress of waiting for the rest of their team to arrive. This went on for a while then Sophia saw Merlin come walking back from his daily task to the watchtower. Every day Merlin walked back to the same place Gunther took them when fleeing from the enemy. He climbed that same tree and watched to see if he could see any signs of Lamorak and the others. It was no different today; he looked so disheartened it made Sophie feel bad.

"Hi Merlin, still no sign of anyone?"

"No Sophia, nothing. I think we should talk about leaving tomorrow and having Gunther fly us to our destination. It will take a lot longer for anyone to ride a horse or walk there, so we will have plenty of time to look for Gunther's family. What do you think?" Merlin asked her.

"I think it's a good idea, Merlin. Maybe we just missed them because they didn't come this way through the woods."

"True, so we need to depart in the morning. It looks like Gunther and Kanani are having a lot of fun. They deserve it."

"I agree Merlin. Come sit next to me and talk. We can start dinner soon."

"Alright." With that Merlin sat down next to her so they could plan their next move.

In the morning they gathered their supplies and scrambled onto Gunther.

"Gunther let's fly back a bit and over the road to see if we can find anyone in our group." Said Merlin.

"Ok, I can do that, is everyone ready?" asked Gunther.

"Yes, Kanani and I are all ready, Merlin is aboard too, so lets go Gunther." Sophia said.

"Ready for takeoff, Gunther is going," he said.

He flew them back to the edge of the forest; they searched the ground under them and saw no one. Then he flew over the dirt road winding through the thick forest for a long time and still they saw nothing. Sophia was so disappointed but knew in her heart they had to go on. She had lost her phone, the only communication with the outside world. They were truly on their own in a century from long ago.

Gunther then turned and flew over the forest so they would be protected from anyone seeking to harm them, and headed for Scotland. That night they got into what is now known as Ayr; on the western border of Scotland; along the shore of the Firth of Clyde. It was beautiful! They found a cave to sleep in acing the water. Merlin got them some food and they camped that night with no fire. They didn't want to attract any attention to themselves. Sophia was so happy they had not encountered any enemies. In the early morning hours, barely twilight, they heard noises.

"Shh," said Merlin as he got up and crept out towards the cave entrance. He motioned for Sophia to come to him. She groggily got up and looked out.

There were Trolls walking through the area!

24

SOPHIA CREPT back and woke Gunther, she told him what was happening. He was scared, but let Kanani and her get on him, Merlin got on the back end of Gunther. The brave dragon crept out of the cave, a Troll saw them and started throwing rocks at them, it made some loud noises and then the Troll's friends came running up behind him to attack them too! Merlin grabbed his wand from his robe, pointed it at the Troll in front, said something, and he turned to stone! Then he did the same to the next one. The rest of the Trolls turned and ran in terror!

"Merlin will they stay that way?" Sophia asked him.

"For eternity, I hope! We need to get far from here as quickly as possible before anything else happens!" He explained. It was just turning daylight as they left on their journey.

~~~~~~

"Look up there!" Screamed Perceval as he pointed at the white dragon in the sky ahead of them.

"That's Gunther with Sophie, Kanani and Merlin!" Shouted Lamorak.

All the men yelled at the Dragon and sped up on their tired horses. It was to no avail; they were too far behind them and could not be heard. At least they knew they were alive and well. Now only if they could make better time.

~~~~~

25

GUNTHER FLEW all day until Sophia insisted he find a safe place to land and take a break. So, he found a place to land in the town of Arbroath on the east border of Scotland about 150 miles northeast of Ayr. They landed on the beach, Merlin went to find some water and Gunther jumped with Kanani into the ocean to get refreshed. Sophia walked around; it was a sandy beach, with magnificent sandstone cliffs stretching out all around them. Sophia kicked off her shoes and walked on the sandy beach letting the waves wash over her feet. She smelled the clean sea air and grabbed a stick, then threw it for Kanani to fetch.

Yipppee! I love chasing sticks, I love water!

Gunther was happy too! How she loved that dragon. Merlin came back with good news, not far from where they were a small stream flowed with fresh drinking water. They followed him there and everyone got a large drink of water. Sophia pulled out some food that they still had and they had a lite snack. Gunther caught a fish and ate that.

"Do you feel like traveling anymore today Gunther or should we stop here for the night?" Sophia asked the dragon.

"I'm a bit tired, could we stay here tonight?" Gunther pleaded.

"Merlin, what do you think?" Sophia asked.

"Let's stay here for the night, Sophia. Then we can have a fresh start in the morning, we've travelled a great distance today and I know we're tired."

"I agree, it's settled then. Let's set up a little camp site for the night." Sophia said, and then got up to start setting up camp.

"I can catch more fish," said Gunther.

"Good, Merlin can you find some herbs for us eat or do you want wood duty?" she asked.

"You go get the herbs Sophia and I will do the fire." said Merlin.

"That's a deal, Kanani you can come with me. I'll meet all of you back here soon." With that Kanani and Sophia took off looking for herbs.

~~~~~~

Lamorak, Perceval, Accalon and Lancelot had been riding their horses all day. They were exhausted and Lamorak was sick with worry for Gunther, Sophia, Kanani and Merlin. Merlin could at least take care of them a bit, but they were so far ahead and would get to Gunther's homeland weeks before any of them could get there. They had been lucky to not run into any more rival knights. Lamorak didn't know how long that luck would run for them. They stopped and camped about the same time Gunther, Sophia, Kanani and Merlin did.

~~~~~~

Grandpa, Jackie Lee, Guinevere, and Morgan went through time. Jackie Lee was jumping up and down running all around. Guinevere was laughing, it was so good to be back, and Jackie Lee was way too funny.

"Ok, what do we do now? There is no transportation." Grandpa said.

"Well, Lamorak's Castle is a short walk from here. We can make it there and hopefully get some horses or a carriage to Camelot." Said Guinevere.

"We need to look out for those Dark Bandits, Father Anderson." Morgan Le Fay warned Grandpa.

"Yes, Sophia told me all about them. Hopefully Lamorak scared them off for a while." Grandpa said.

"I hope so," said Guinevere.

With that they walked in the direction of Lamorak's castle.

~~~~~~

Casey Lane rode ahead of the King and his knights. Jennie and Leila rode beside her. They arrived where the attack had happened.

"Look at the graves!" Leila pointed as she screamed in horror!

"Oh no," said Jennie, "I hope it isn't any of our men!"

"Well, it has to be," said Richard riding up and jumping off his horse. "The enemy would have taken their dead with them. Our men weren't going home, they would have had to bury them."

Casey Lane jumped off her horse too, they looked around. There had been a horrible battle. She followed the hoof prints from the horses. There was something hiding behind a bush. She reached down and pulled out a phone!

Then she went running back to the others.

"Look what I found!" Exclaimed Casey Lane excitedly!

"Oh, no!" Screamed Jennie putting her hands to her mouth. "That's Sophie's!"

Richard came over and put his arm around Jennie. "I'm sure she's ok, honey." He tried to comfort his wife.

King Arthur rode up.

"This is not good; men you need to dig up those graves. We need to see who's in there." He instructed his knights.

The knights jumped off their horses and went over to the graves.

"Not a pleasant task," said one of the knights.

"No, but we need to just get it done," said another.

They dug up the graves and then King Arthur went over to look inside them. He took count of which knights he had lost and said a prayer.

Casey Lane came up behind them and glanced in the graves too. Then she turned and walked back to Jennie.

"Sophie isn't there, so she's alive," said Casey Lane.

"Thank goodness!" Sobbed Jennie with relief.

The graves were covered back up and King Arthur ordered everyone to continue forward. No way were they going to camp here tonight.

26

THE NEXT morning Sophia begrudgingly left this oasis with her party. As Gunther flew them out she looked down at the sandy beach and sea cliffs. Wow, I could live here, she thought to herself, they flew all day and landed in Loch Ness that evening. Sophia made sure they stayed away from the water; she didn't want to meet any hideous sea monsters tonight!

~~~~~~

Lamorak, Perceval, Accalon, and Lancelot were now riding through Ayr.

"Well, look at that!" exclaimed Lamorak.

"Yes, Merlin has been here for sure!" Laughed Perceval.

"Let's pass quickly before any more trolls not turned to stone show up!" Shouted Accalon.

They made their horses go swiftly through the stone trolls and ended up near Glasgow that night.

~~~~~~

Grandpa, Jackie Lee, Morgan Le Fay, and Guinevere arrived at Lamorak's castle.

"Thank goodness the drawbridge is down," exclaimed Guinevere!

"Yes, I don't want to walk all the way to Camelot!" Said Morgan Le Fay.

They entered the courtyard and walked over to the stable.

"Hello, anyone around?" Asked Guinevere.

"Yes, hello," said a stable hand as he walked out to see what they wanted. He saw it was the Queen and dropped to his knees.

A kitchen hand was walking back into the kitchen when she noticed the crowd and realized it was the Queen.

"The Queen is here!" She shouted as she ran into the kitchen.

Everyone dropped what they were doing and ran out into the courtyard to see the Queen.

"I heard she's been missing," said one maid.

"Well look who she's with and look at that dog! He's wearing armor!" She giggled.

"Please get up," said Guinevere to the stable boy. "We need some horses or a carriage to get us Camelot tonight.

He got up and said, "the carriages have all been taken, but we have an open carriage in the back. Would that do?"

"Yes, that will be fine," Morgan Le Fay said rather tartly. She was getting impatient.

"Guinevere are you going with us to catch up to the King or are you going back to Camelot to stay?" Asked Grandpa.

"I want to go with you to find Arthur," she said.

"Morgan, what about you?" Asked Grandpa.

"Well, I'm not going to miss out on any fun!" she answered.

"Ok, then why don't I call Jennie and see where they are. I won't let them know I'm here, so we can surprise them." Grandpa told them.

"That's a great idea!" Guinevere said; she was getting excited.

"Well, let's leave here and I'll call. I don't want to draw any more attention to ourselves. If they have left on the trip, is there a short cut for us, so we don't have to go to Camelot?" he asked.

"Yes, we can take another road that goes north of Camelot and will save us a lot of time if we are going to Scotland." said Guinevere.

The carriage was brought out and the horses were hitched up. The kitchen maids loaded the carriage with baskets of food and water. The stable hand put enough oats in the back for the horses to keep them for a week. It was a huge carriage, so it could carry everything. They rode out of the castle and an hour later came to a fork in the road.

"Ok, let's pull up here," Grandpa said, they were at the intersection of either going to Camelot or taking the short cut to Scotland.

Ring ring, "Hello," said Jennie surprised to find her phone ringing.

"Hello dear, this is Grandpa," he said.

"Hi Grandpa, what's up?" asked Jennie.

"I was just wondering where you are dear? Have you started on your journey?" asked Grandpa.

"Yes, we're almost in Scotland," she answered.

"I will check in with you from time to time dear. Stay safe and let me know when you find your sister." He said.

"Ok, Grandpa, I will. You take care too. I love you," she said.

"Good bye dear, I love you too." With that he hung up with a grin on his face.

"This is going to be fun!" Exclaimed Guinevere joyfully, jumping up and hugging Grandpa.

"Yes, it is!" Grandpa beamed.

Jackie Lee barked, and Morgan rolled her eyes and laughed.

~~~~~~

"I'm going back home!" Cundrie pouted, showing her anger and disgust to Iago. She was sitting next to a dumpster they had just rummaged through for scraps of food. They were behind a row of restaurants in down town Luxembourg.

"I don't think we had it this bad at home. Will I still have a job though?" Asked Iago.

"If I still have a marriage you will." She said tartly. She got up and dusted off her dirty skirt. Come on let's start walking to the caves.

Iago got up and followed her, feeling low about the situation they were in.

~~~~~~

27

FROM LOCH NESS the next day Sophia and her party made it into the Northern Highlands.

"Are you getting close to home Gunther?" She asked the dragon when they stopped for a quick break.

"Yes, I believe so, aren't we Merlin?" asked Gunther.

"Looking at this map, I believe so. We need to go to the very tip of the Northern Highlands. Your family should be on one of the Orkney Islands. King Arthur found you as a baby in the Northern Highlands. Your parents were killed and taken by men that wanted to wipe all of you out. We saved you, I believe your remaining family would have moved as far north as they could for safety." Merlin replied.

"Well then we are almost there!" Sophia exclaimed with excitement. "Will they accept Kanani and me?" she asked.

"I think that Gunther and I should approach them first, Sophie. We will leave you on the mainland for a short while until we know it's safe." Said Merlin.

"NO!" Cried Gunther despairingly! "Sophie and Kanani must come with me!"

"Gunther, Merlin will protect you!" Sophia told him.

"You will be alone though, and something could hurt you!" Gunther cried.

She went over and gave that silly dragon a hug. "I love you too Gunther." she said.

"I love you too!" Gunther sobbed.

Sophie has me Gunther, I will protect her.

"Come on let's not waste good daylight," said Merlin.

"Ok," I said, "let's go Gunther."

Gunther got up and lowered himself, so they could all scamper up on him.

Gunther flew for a few more hours and then landed along the coastline for the night. Tomorrow they would reach the tip of the land, Dunnet Head, towards their destination.

~~~~~~

Lamorak and the knights made it to Clyde River that night. They sat up camp and took turns keeping watch. In the middle of the night ugly trolls attacked them!

28

"WE'RE FINALLY here!" Sophia shouted with joy!

"I am so excited!" Stated Gunther nervously.

"Ok, why don't we land and walk around to find a good place to leave Sophie and Kanani, Gunther." Said Merlin.

Gunther landed; there were beautiful white sand beaches with limestone cliffs at Dunnet Head.

"Oh, look there's a huge cave, Merlin! Can we check it out?" Sophie asked him.

"Let me go first in case something lives in it Sophie." said Merlin.

He climbed down the cliff and proceeded to check out the cave. He was gone a long time. Then he appeared with a grin on his face just as Sophie was starting to get worried.

"It's empty, follow me." He said gesturing to follow him.

Kanani bounded down ahead of Merlin and Sophia climbed down behind him. Gunther flew and beat them all there. Beautiful eagles were flying around them. It was gorgeous here, but Sophie knew the weather in winter was cold.

"Kanani and I will be fine here Merlin. Do you want to stay one night or go over to the Islands right away?" she asked.

"I think we should go take a quick look and come back for you tonight Sophie. This cave is empty now, but who knows what animal lives here at night." he said.

"Then please go and hurry back," she said as she walked over to Gunther and kissed his face. "You'll be ok Gunther, I love you." she told him.

"I love you too," Gunther replied.

With that Gunther and Merlin took off and left Kanani and Sophia on the beach. They arrived on the little island of South Roanaldsay a short time later.

Gunther landed with Merlin and they looked around. Suddenly a white dragon came forward to see who had come for a visit. There were ten dragons, counting a baby dragon.

A big dragon came forward, the others stayed back.

"I'm Drake, who are you?" he asked Gunther.

"I'm Gunther, I live with King Arthur and this is his wizard, Merlin."

"Gunther!" Shouted Drake, your alive! I didn't recognize!" He bounded forward to hug Gunther. Merlin jumped off to get out of the way.

All the dragons introduced themselves to Gunther; Merlin took out his looking glass to check on Sophia and Kanani. To his horror he saw two big black dragons with something in their claws!

29

SOPHIA WAS watching Gunther and Merlin disappear. He wasn't paying attention to Kanani barking when she was attacked from above! A big ugly black dragon grabbed Sophia and another one snatched Kanani. Sophia started screaming while Kanani was barking and struggling.

Let me go you big bird! This is not supposed to happen!

Merlin left the dragons to use his eyepiece to check on Sophia and Kanani. He saw what happened and was horrified.

Merlin raced back to Gunther and shouted to all of the Dragons that he saw a black dragon grab Sophia and another one grabbed Kanani. They needed to go get them now!

"Ok, let's go kick some black dragons around and save our friends! Gunther you stay back with baby Fafnir and Merlin!" Drake shouted as they took off to save them.

"I'm not staying here, hop on Merlin. Fafnir stay with your mom." With that Gunther and Merlin took off behind the big white dragons.

Drake reached the dragon holding Sophia and attacked him from above.

When that happened Sophia was let go so the black dragon could fight back. Sophia plunged to the ground but was saved by some brush and the fact that the black dragon was not too far airborne yet. Then another white dragon attacked the one holding Kanani. She dropped down next to Sophia. Sophia grabbed Kanani's collar and they ran as fast as they could in the opposite direction. Then they saw Gunther approaching.

"Sophie and Kanani, I'm coming for you!" Shouted Gunther so they could hear him. I knew you would, Gunther. Hurry! Kanani started barking.

Gunther made a quick landing and they climbed onto him. Merlin helped Sophia get on Gunther and then helped Kanani. As they took off they looked at the battle, the white dragons were winning. They flew back to the island and landed. The female dragons gathered around inquiring for their wellbeing. They couldn't believe what they had been through and neither could Sophia.

If they only knew what she and Kanani had really been through they would have been truly amazed. Sophia was wondering why she was here again. Thinking perhaps her thinking had been a bit off when she decided to come back in time once more.

It was hours before the male dragons came back. The female dragons had food out and Merlin made a huge bon fire to keep the humans warm that evening. There was a chill in the air as they sat around for most of the night talking. It was decided that they needed to stay here until backup knights arrived. The other hope was that King Arthur had gotten wind of their dire situation and would come to save them. The dragons were apprehensive at first to leave this place until Gunther convinced them they would be safer and happier with a life in

Camelot. Sophia just kept thinking about the caves being prepared for them behind the town, hoping there would be enough of them for the ten dragons and Gunther too. How she loved that dragon! She could never go back to the future and leave him behind.

30

A BIG ugly smelly four-foot troll came stomping into camp. Lamorak pulled out his sword and swung at him. Perceval jumped up out of a light sleep and got behind him. The troll turned to face Perceval, and Lamorak swung his sword slashing his right arm. The troll screamed and grabbed his nearly severed arm turning to glare at Lamorak. Perceval used this opportunity to finish him off. Then there came two more trolls looking like the first one wanting to kill the men.

Then there came two more trolls looking like the first one wanting to kill the men. This battle went on for an hour, when it was finished the brave knights were exhausted. At least they were all alive; the trolls had all been killed. The camp was a disaster, so they decided to pick up what they could and leave right away. It was now early evening and they arrived in Saint Andrews, they decided to rest up and eat. Tomorrow would be another long day, but they should be safe tonight. There were people around and a small village.

~~~~~~

They would be able to get some supplies that they had lost last night and stock up for the rest of the journey.

Grandpa, Jackie Lee, Guinevere, and Morgan were making good time. They had not run into any trouble, and the short cut should bring them above the others. The King's party was so large they must be moving slow.

They got onto the main road going into Scotland.

"Now we are either behind them or ahead," Grandpa told the others. "Let's camp here by the stream tonight and see if we hear anything in either direction tomorrow morning."

"I agree," said Guinevere, "I'm tired of riding in this carriage all day. She stopped the horses and they got out. Jackie Lee jumped out and went over to the water gulping it down. Grandpa unhooked the horses, got them watered and fed. Morgan actually made a place for them to eat and started a fire. They spent a pleasant uneventful evening; they didn't know how lucky they were, because they were just below the place that Merlin had turned the trolls into stone. They calculated that the King's band must be behind them, they had taken quite a short cut. They waited another day and then it happened.

~~~~~~

They heard voices and horses. Jackie Lee took off running fast towards the noise.

Casey Lane thought she heard Jackie Lee. She was riding next to Jennie. "Did you hear that?" She asked Jennie.

"Yes, that's strange. There aren't any ~~~~~~ dogs with us." Jennie said.

Jackie Lee had spotted Casey and was barking his head off running as fast as his legs and body armor would let him. Casey! Here I am, see me? I found you, I found you!

~~~~~~

"Oh my gosh! That's Jackie Lee!" Screamed Casey Lane jumping off her horse and running to greet her dog.

When they met, Jackie Lee jumped up to greet her, as she bent over to pet him, he started licking her face.

"How did you find me? What a clever boy, I'm so happy to see you!" Casey Lane was beside herself with joy.

"Look, there's Grandpa too!" Screamed Jennie as she ran to hug her grandfather.

Guinevere stopped the horses and Grandpa jumped off taking after Jackie Lee. For such an elderly man he was still in pretty good shape.

"Grandpa! How did you find us? I can't believe you're here!" Cried Jennie finally reaching him and giving him a big hug.

"Jackie Lee and I could not stay away from this adventure, and neither could Morgan or Guinevere."

"Grandpa, that's awesome!" Jennie cried. Leila and Richard came running up to greet the newcomers too. They were all talking and hugging when King Arthur approached, everyone stopped talking and held their breath.

"Your Highness, your Queen awaits you," Grandpa told him with a twinkle in his eye.

"I see her, excuse me," King Arthur said as he took off to greet his wife.

He approached the carriage. "My Lady I have missed you." He said.

"I never want to leave you again, my King. Please forgive me, I have missed you too." Guinevere stepped out of the carriage and the King lifted her up to sit in front of him on his horse.

It was such a great reunion for all involved; they stayed there that evening.

They talked into the night then decided how they were going to proceed on this quest.

31

CUNDRIE AND IAGO finally made it back to the caves. It was a long unpleasant journey that tired them both. Cundrie was in a foul mood and took it out on Iago.

"Ok, here we are." Cundrie said and gave Iago an exasperated look. "This is enough adventure for me, I will go first."

"That is fine, go ahead and I will be behind you."

With that Cundrie went through the portal and landed on the other side. She looked around, she was so happy to be back. She hoped that Accalon would not be too unhappy with her. Iago kept his word and came through a few minutes later.

"Ok," Cundrie looked at Iago, "We need to start walking to the castle before it gets dark."

"I don't know if I should go back, in fact I think I will go in the other direction." He started walking away from her.

"Oh no you don't! I did not get into this mess alone and I will not face Accalon or Yglais alone!" She was glaring at his disappearing back. "At least walk me back, so I am not alone!" She pleaded with some desperation in her voice.

He turned around. "Ok, I will walk you back, but I do not know if I shall stay."

"Good enough, I guess. Let us start off now." She said with relief in her voice.

He turned around, came back to her and they walked off side by side, not saying a word. After an hour they saw the castle. Cundrie was getting butterflies in her stomach with anxiety. Little did she know that Yglais, Accalon, Perceval, and Lamorak were not in Camelot. She did not have anything to be afraid of yet. They got closer and her mouth fell open.

"I can not believe this! Look, the drawbridge is up. We can not enter the castle!" Cundrie exclaimed.

"It is never up except at night, or if there is danger." He looked around. "We had better find cover before night comes. I wonder what is going on?"

"I don't know. I have an uneasy feeling. Perhaps we should get back on the road and keep walking towards Camelot. What do you think?" She asked him.

"Yes, we need to get out of here." He said, "First let us walk around the outside of the castle. I know another way in if it's unlocked."

"You do?" Cundrie asked. "Who else knows about this?"

"Merlin, I saw him using it one time when he was visiting. He did not see me watching him. Follow me and I will show you where it is." He turned and starting walking clockwise around the outside wall of the castle. The only problem was the moat around the castle. They would have to cross that first.

"What do you expect me to do?" Cundrie huffed at Iago. "Wade through that mucky infested water?"

"Do you have another idea? Really Cundrie this is not as bad as eating out of dumpsters." He kept walking around the outside of the moat glancing at the castle wall for the opening. She had to walk fast to keep up with him.

She thought that eating out of dumpsters was pretty disgusting when you were hungry, but it just might be beneath her to get in that murky water.

"Ok, there," he pointed, "Do you see the outline of the door?"

She squinted. "Yes, how do we know if we can enter through it?"

"We don't until we try." he said. "I will get into the water and go across. If it is unlocked, I will come back and help you through the moat, ok?"

"Do I have a choice?" Cundrie sulked.

"Not unless you want to be a sitting target unprotected out here all night." He tossed off his jacket and removed his shoes.

She watched him wade in about 8 feet or so then it was really deep and he had to swim across the middle portion until he could wade out of the muddy water.

He made it to the other side. He got onto the bank and turned around throwing his hands in the air.

"See nothing ate me and I made it. You can do this too. Let me check the door." He shouted across the water.

He went over to the door and pushed on it. To his relief it swung open. He stepped inside. This passageway ran beneath the courtyard, under the castle coming out into the kitchen. He was satisfied they could get through or at least hide in here tonight until the castle was accessible in the morning. He stepped back out and swam back across to Cundrie.

"Ok, grab my hand and let's go." He said pulling her into the water.

"Oh, I hate this! The dumpster is fine dining compared to this." She moaned but followed him.

They made it across. She got out behind him and wrung out her dress then followed him through the door.

They walked through a long dark damp tunnel; she knew there were rats; she could hear their squeals and scuffling along the floor.

It seemed like forever before they came to stairs leading up. They reached the top of the 100 steps and there was another long staircase no different from the previous one.

"Do you know for sure where this ends up?"

"I have done this one other time and it comes out in the pantry of the main kitchen." He told her.

"Good, maybe we can get something decent to eat when we get there." She was really wet and cold, but above all she was famished. They had not had a decent meal in weeks. They should have stayed with the others at the monastery. Better yet, they should have never gone. "

Too late for that kind of thinking now. She thought out loud.

"Did you say something?" Iago asked.

"Ah no, just talking to myself she sharply said, while thinking the only intelligent conversation is one with herself."

"Ok, look there's the entrance up ahead." He hurried his steps.

"Thank goodness, I am worn out." She could hardly take another step.

Iago opened the door, there was no lock on it and they stepped through. The cooks were in the kitchen just sitting down with the hired help to eat. They saw Cundrie and Iago. Jumping to their feet, three of the women ran over to hug them.

"We have been so worried about the two of you. The Queen came through here not that long ago, we wondered where the two of you had gone." Said Ivis, the Head Cook.

"Come dear, sit by the fire," she grabbed Cundrie and walked her over to the open fire. Another servant grabbed two chairs. Both Cundrie and Iago were placed by the fire to dry out and given a big bowl of hot stew with homemade bread to eat.

"Is Sir Accalon or Lady Yglais here?" asked Cundrie.

"No, Lady Yglais is still at Camelot overseeing the houses being built. Sir Perceval, Sir Lamorak, and Sir Accalon went on a quest and never returned. So, King Arthur has a party going after them as we speak. There is no telling when they will return." said Ivis.

"They never returned? This is terrible!" Cundrie cried.

"Yes, it is. They left to seek the last of the white dragons, to save them from extinction," added Afawen the maid.

"I must get to Camelot tomorrow," Cundrie said, "If anything has happened to Accalon I will never forgive myself for having left." She finished her stew and placed her dish in the sink. "Thank you for feeding me. I need to go to my room and get cleaned up. Please have a bath prepared. I will see all of you in the morning. Iago, take care and go to the stable. I will need a horse in the morning and I would appreciate it if you got my white horse ready by eight a.m."

"Yes, my Lady, I will have her ready. However, you cannot ride to Camelot alone." He looked around.

"I will go with you, my Lady," said Afawen. "Bryn went with Lady Sophia and I am not needed here. I can at least help Lady Yglais' maids get them settled in the new house. The plan is for us to take turns living in Camelot and running this castle."

"Good, I will ride with you too then," said Iago. "If anyone else is wanting to go, be at the stable early in the morning, so we can prepare the trip." With that he thanked them for the food and left.

32

CASEY LANE and Jackie Lee were riding ahead of the King's entourage. Jackie Lee started barking so Casey caught up to him to see what he was making such a fuss about.

"Jackie Lee, come here," she called getting off the horse.

Jennie was right behind her with Richard. They got off their horses as well and walked over to take a look at what was setting Jackie Lee off.

"What are they?" Asked Casey Lane.

"They look like stone trolls," said Richard. "Ha, Merlin must have been this way. He would not have left Sophia or Kanani, so I bet they're alright Jennie."

"I hope your right, Richard. How horrifying these trolls must be when alive!" Jennie was disgusted and walked away.

The Kings' party arrived and had a look around. It was decided that they should try to move on tonight and find a safer place to camp.

~~~~~~

Weeks had gone by and everyday Merlin looked through his eyeglass to see if anyone was coming for them. Then one morning he saw something!

33

MERLIN RAN back to get Gunther's attention.

"Sophia, Gunther, I just saw some knights. We need to go over to the mainland and have a look."

"Come on Gunther, let us get on you so we can go see who found us!" Sophia was so happy she wanted to jump for joy but climbed onto Gunther instead. Of course, Kanani had to go too, so Merlin helped her get aboard, then he got on and off they flew over the water.

The men were looking around and then noticed Gunther.

"Look, I think that's Gunther!" Shouted Perceval, he was thrilled!

"It is, there's Sophia and Kanani!" Lamorak shouted as he jumped off his horse.

Gunther flew over them. "It's our knights! You can land Gunther." Merlin instructed the dragon.

Gunther circled and landed by the men.

Sophia jumped off Gunther and Kanani did too following behind her.

"I can't believe you found us! I'm so happy!" She ran over forgetting her dignity and hugged each of the Knights.

"We are happier to see you," exclaimed Lamorak. "We have had a rough journey, it looks like you did too. We saw the stone trolls and the dead dragons. I'm amazed to see all of you alive. How did you defeat the black dragons?"

"We had help." Sophia continued relating the adventure they had along the way to find the white dragons."

"Where are the rest of you?" asked Merlin.

"They were killed, Merlin. It was a horrible battle. How many dragons have you found?" Lamorak asked.

"There are ten dragons, eleven with Gunther."

"Well that's too many dragons for us to take to Camelot alone. There are too many dangers."

"Lamorak, you four cannot stay here either unless the dragons come over here. Black dragons guard these beaches at night."

"Perhaps we should get the dragons to move over here," Perceval told them.

"Yes, I think that is the best idea," said Lamorak.

"Ok, then it's decided, if we can convince them. Let's talk to Gunther." Merlin turned around and walked over to Gunther giving him the men's suggestion.

"Ok, let's go back and talk to Drake and the others," agreed Gunther.

"Sophia, you and Kanani stay over here. Gunther and I will return with an answer or with dragons. Why don't you find a good place for eleven dragons and all of us," Merlin offered?

Sophia turned around and spoke to Lamorak. "There's Smoo Cave down below us. I would love to explore it. I think it's big enough for all the dragons and us too. That way we will have protection from the black dragons and plenty of food from the sea."

"That is an excellent idea. Can you show us where it is?" he asked her.

"Yes, just follow Kanani and me." Sophia started leading the way.

Lamorak turned back around, "Perceval, you and the others can follow us with your horses." Then he turned back around leading his horse behind Kanani down the trail.

We got down to the beach and approached the cave.

"Stay here Sophia, let us check out the cave first and make sure that there aren't any dragons living in it." Lamorak said.

"Ok, but I'm pretty sure it will be ok. The white dragons had a battle with them and won. The black dragons haven't been seen around since." Sophia told him.

The men left their horses outside and walked into the cave. Upon entering they saw what a wide cave it was, the chamber they walked into was about forty to fifty feet high, one hundred fifty feet long and a little more than 100 feet wide. This would be an excellent place to house all of them, even throughout the winter. They came out a bit later and Lamorak had a grin on his face.

"It is a grand cave, Sophia. You can get Kanani settled here. We will arrange for the horses to eat and start a fire.

Perceval is already getting set up to catch some fish for our dinner."

"Fabulous! Come on Kanani!"

Ok, Sophie, this is fun! Can we eat now?

By the time they saw Gunther flying back with Merlin with other dragons flying behind him, they had a warm fire going. Dinner was made; a place for the dragons was set up in the cave.

There was a great introduction between the men and dragons.

~~~~~~

Cundrie, Iago and Afawen arrived in Camelot. Lady Yglais ran over to great them. She didn't know if she was angry with Cundrie or glad to see her. Cundrie was also apprehensive about the meeting. Lady Yglais interrogated both Cundrie and Iago until she was satisfied, and then laughed from relief. She had feared the worse for both of them. Iago was allowed to stay for now. They were to wait until Accalon arrived, if he came back alive it would be his decision. In the meantime, Iago was put to work getting the homes and caves ready for the hopeful return of the dragons and people.

~~~~~~

The Kings men were getting closer to the cave where Sophia and the Dragons were staying. They didn't know it though and with winter coming upon them the King feared they would be stuck with no shelter or food. They needed to get there soon or find a town to stay in and wait out winter

~~~~~~

The dragons were doing well sleeping with the humans in the cave at night. By day they went up the cliff, played, caught food and looked for any help coming to get them.

"Sir Lamorak," said Sophia, "I really want to explore this cave. I've checked and there are several tunnels and chambers. It would be fun to see where each of them go. Tomorrow Kanani and I are going exploring. I just wanted you to know so that you don't worry about us."

"Thank you for telling me, however I do not think it is safe for a Lady to go off on her own. Perceval and I will accompany you and Kanani." He was determined not to let Sophia out of site after that attack of the black dragons and not knowing what was in the tunnels.

"Great, do you think you should ask Perceval first though?" Sophia was being smart.

"Yes, I suppose I should," Lamorak laughed. "Come with me, let us find him and see if he will go on the mission quest with us."

With that Lamorak called Kanani and they climbed the cliff looking for Perceval.

Perceval and Lancelot were practicing swords fights. The dragons were cheering for one or the other of them. They had to keep themselves in shape.

It was agreed that the next day Perceval, Lancelot, Accalon, Sophia and Kanani would explore the caves. Merlin preferred to stay back and work on some magic, protecting the dragons too, in case any black dragons approached.

"After this Sophia, we must prepare for winter. I do not think any of the King's men will get here before the cold winds and temperatures arrive." Lamorak was looking a bit worried about this.

"Ok, I promise that I will help us get everything ready after this venture." Sophia agreed excitedly.

Smoo Cave is a very large sea cave; it has a cave river running through it and lies at the inner end of a narrow inlet with Durness Limestone. The layers in this formation are layers of limestone and dolomites. The birds she had seen in the cave were rockdoves, they nested in the higher chambers of the cave. There were starlings living in the holes within the rocks. There were wrens and blackbirds living at the cave mouth plus numerous other creatures. They had been eating a lot of rabbit lately. Sophie knew they couldn't live on just rabbit. They needed to find other sources of food, perhaps there were fish in the river. She was anxious to see the cave river she remembered reading about years ago. Sophia had a special love of caves and had done a thesis paper in college on the most famous caves around the world.

The next morning, they got ready and explored through one of the tunnels. It was dark at first then they heard gushing water. They came into a massive cavern dimly lit with phosphorescence. They could just make out a pool of fresh water and a waterfall coming from above out of the limestone walls.

"Look, fresh water for us!" Sophia chased Kanani over to the water. Kanani barked and jumped in splashing all around. Yippee, water! Everyone started laughing, this was a good sign that they had some fresh water now.

"We will have to figure a way to get this water to all of us daily, it's too narrow in here for the dragons to get through the passageway. Let us move on and see what other wonders we can find in here."

Lamorak led them out of this cavern back into the passageway.

They came to another cavern and it too had running water, which ran into the cave river she knew was here.

"This is what I wanted to find," she told the others.

"Wow, if we had a boat we could go down the river and see where it comes out." Accalon said.

"We might have plenty of time to build one if no one comes to help escort the dragons home soon," Lamorak answered him.

They spent a whole day walking down one passageway, before they knew it the day was drifting into evening and they needed to get back. Little did they know what they had missed that day, but they were about to find out.

34

THEY HEARD them before they saw them.

"Gunther come here please?" Merlin asked the dragon. "I sense someone approaching. Could you see who is coming please?"

"Yes, Gunther is a good dragon, I will be back." Gunther said as he took flight.

~~~~~~

"Look, that's Gunther!" Shouted Jennie to Casey Lane and Richard.

"So, it is! Fantastic, we made it!" Shouted Richard.

Jennie, Casey Lane, Jackie Lee and Richard let the King know. King Arthur was so relieved to finally arrive at their destination.

~~~~~~

Gunther saw them and flew back to Merlin. The dragons were all lined up with Merlin in front as the King's party approached. Jackie Lee was introduced to the dragons, so he didn't chase them. Sophia, Kanani and the others came out of the cave in time for the arrival of the King's party. They were greeted warmly by everyone! Sophia and Casey Lane shook hands; Kanani and Jackie Lee chased each other. There was so much going on with all of the additional people. The King had his soldiers get water out of the cave; they had a lot of food and supplies, so they set up camp above the cave. Only the dragons would sleep in the cave from now on. They decided to bear out winter here and next spring they would make the long trip back to Camelot.

The winter passed, they made it through safely. Spring arrived so they started the long trip back to Camelot. Early summer was approaching when they reached their home. Word got around that the King was approaching. The King's people lined the pathway as King Arthur and his party approached. The people cheered and danced! A festival took place in honor of the dragons and the safe return of the King. This was a very long and successful quest.

The dragons were all given caves. Gunther had his cave closest to Sophia and Kanani.

"It's been a lot of fun," said Casey Lane. "Jackie Lee and I need to go home though."

"I understand, it was nice of you to come. I can't get over Jackie Lee convincing Grandpa to bring him through time. I will never stop chuckling about that." Sophia laughed.

"I know, Jackie Lee is quite the character." Casey Lane told her. It was so nice of your Grandpa to have me start calling him that too."

"I know, he is a dear," said Sophie.

Grandpa approached the women.

"I will go back with you my dear. You need to get your belongings from Sophia's house and then I will take you both to the airport after I pay you."

"Ok, sounds good to Jackie Lee and me." Casey Lane looked at Grandpa agreeing.

Grandpa turned to Sophia and Jennie, "I plan on coming back over here to live and open a Catholic Church. I'm going to become a Priest instead of a Monk. It will take a bit of time, but not much. Could you get the church built and a rectory for me?" He asked them.

"Yes, that's fantastic, Grandpa!" Sophia hugged him, Jennie got into the bear hug as well.

"Sophia and I will make sure it gets done, Grandpa, hurry back to us. I love you." Jennie said.

"I love all of you too, I will be back within the month." Grandpa then boarded the carriage with Casey Lane and Jackie Lee.

Bye, Jackie Lee, come back and see me sometime. It's been fun having another German Shepherd to talk to. Kanani told him.

Bye, Kanani. You're a fun girl too. This has been a grand time. I hope to visit again someday. Jackie Lee gave Kanani a lick and jumped into the carriage with Casey Lane and Grandpa.

The girls watched until the carriage was out of sight.

"Well, we have a lot more to do little sister. Let's get going." Jennie walked off to talk to the builders.

Sophia's house was done and so were Susan and Kimo's. They were cobblestone houses, with a kitchen, fireplace, living room, bathroom and two bedrooms. The roofs were thatch and Lady Yglais had flowers planted all around the front of Sophia's. Lady Yglais had her new place as well; it was much bigger than Sophia's, because she knew her sons would want to stay with her when in Camelot. Sophia found Yglais in the school putting all of Sophia's materials away on new shelves that had been built. School would start in the fall, Jennie and Susan would teach. Sophia decided to teach violin and work with the older children teaching them to read and write. Sophia and Lamorak were very good friends, it was an exciting time in Camelot. Guinevere had sent Lancelot away and the King was very relieved.

35

CASEY LANE, Jackie Lee and Grandpa went through the portal.

"I can't believe no one towed your car after all this time Grandpa."

"I had a monk from the monastery come put a sign in the window saying the car was not abandoned to call their number if it became a problem." Grandpa unlocked the driver's door and took down the sign. Then he unlocked the other doors letting Casey Lane and Jackie Lee in. When they arrived at Sophie's house, Casey Lane ran into the bedroom where her belongings were. Jackie Lee was hot on her heels. She grabbed her cell phone and turned it on.

"Yikes, Jackie Lee. Steven has left a lot of messages. Let's listen to them."

She pressed on the first message.

"Hi Casey, I got your message. Please call me when you and Jackie Lee return. Love Steve."

Message two, "Casey, I still haven't heard anything. I hope you and Jackie Lee are all right. Your house is fine. Please call me soon. Love, Steve."

Message three, "Casey, I'm getting really concerned. I know you are a big girl and know you can take care of yourself, well I think you can. I've got a big decision to make. I would love to discuss it with you. I need to talk to you soon. Please call me! Love, Steve."

Message four, "Casey, this must be some kind of case you're on. I hope Jackie Lee is taking care of you. I had to make the decision on my own. When you two come back here I will be gone. I took the Sheriff's job in a small town in Montana. I will keep this phone number. Please call me when you can. Maybe you and Jackie Lee can come visit me when you return? I love you Casey. Take care. Steve."

"Yikes! Steve moved to Montana Jackie Lee! With the money we made on this assignment we can go back to Seattle and buy an RV and drive to Montana."

That sounds like fun, whatever an RV is. Steve moved to Montana? Wow, I bet your upset Casey. Jackie Lee was thumping his tail and gave her his paw.

"Oh, thank you Jackie Lee." She took his paw and shook it.

~~~~~~

Grandpa walked out to the mailbox and returned to the kitchen. There was a letter from the government of the US State Department to Sophia. He wondered if he should open it and decided to call Sophia instead.

"Hi Grandpa, you made it back ok. I miss you already." Sophia told him.

"Hi dear, yes we made it back. Sophie, I'm calling dear because there is a letter here from the State Department to you. Do you want me to open it and read it you?" He asked her.

"Yes, it could be important."

Grandpa carefully opened it.

Dear Mrs. Sophia Barnes,

We have some news about the missing men from the mission your husband was on. We have found out that some of the men have survived but have been held by the Taliban. We don't want you to get up your hopes that Mr. Barnes is still alive, but it could be a possibility. We have a special investigation going on in this matter. You will be contacted if your husband is found alive. I'm sorry this has been so hard on you and the other families.

Thank you very much,

Colonel McFarland

"Good grief! What should I think?" Sophia asked her Grandpa.

"Don't get your hopes up dear. I will write a letter, with your help, right now to leave here in case John shows up. Then he will know where to find you. I will also leave a phone for him to call you."

"Thank you, Grandpa. I don't know what else we can do." Sophia told him. "I would like the letter to say this:"

Dear John,

If you are reading this letter, I know you are alive and have found your way home. I have loved you since the first time I saw you, I miss you more than you could ever know. My heart has been broken, but I can't hang on forever, Honey. I have an unbelievable story to tell you. In short, I'm with my sister and her husband. I've made a new life here; we are in Camelot. If you are alive, please call me. I will either come back for you or tell you how to find me if it is within 10 years' time. I pray it's you who is reading this.

Your loving wife,

Sophia

Grandpa wrote the letter while Sophie dictated it.

"Ok dear, I'll leave it on the counter. I love you Sophie, I'll check on the house from time to time until I come back."

"Thank you, Grandpa. I love you too. Goodbye for now."

"Goodbye dear." Then he hung up.

"Kanani, John might be alive." She said hopefully to Kanani.

Oh, Sophie don't get your hopes up. Kanani wagged her tail.

"I don't think I will say anything to the others, but I'm going to tell Gunther. Come on Kanani." Sophia got up from her desk and put her manuscript away. Kanani followed Sophia out of the house and over to Gunther's cave.

"Hi Sophie," Gunther came out to greet them. "Hi Kanani."

"Hi Gunther," she said.

Kanani wagged her tale and said in doggie talk, hi Gunther.

"I have come to give you some news. My husband may be alive!" Sophie told him.

"What do you mean might?" He was shocked and a little disappointed. Gunther didn't want to lose Sophie or Kanani.

Then Sophie explained about the letter and what it meant. She told him that it was a secret and Gunther liked that. They then said their goodnights.

~~~~~~

"Let's get our stuff together so Grandpa can take us to the airport, Jackie Lee."

Great I'm ready let's go. Jackie Lee was walking to the bedroom door.

"Wait a minute young man." Casey told him. "You remember what we went through at the Seattle airport with that body armor you insisted on wearing? Off it comes, I'll pack it in my suitcase."

No Casey I like wearing it. Jackie Lee gave Casey the cocked head sad eye look.

"Come here, I'm taking it off. We want to get home without any hassles." She walked over and took his armor off and put in her case. Then she gave Jackie a big kiss on the top of his head.

Ok, I like those kisses. Just this once Casey I will let you have your way. Thump thump thump, went Jackie Lee's tail.

~~~~~~

It was possible to change history, if only in fairy tales. Sophia sat down at her new oak desk and continued writing her story about Camelot and the Dragon. She was writing a book for the school children. She would always wonder now, if someday John would show up. She felt truly blessed to have such a loving family with her in Camelot.

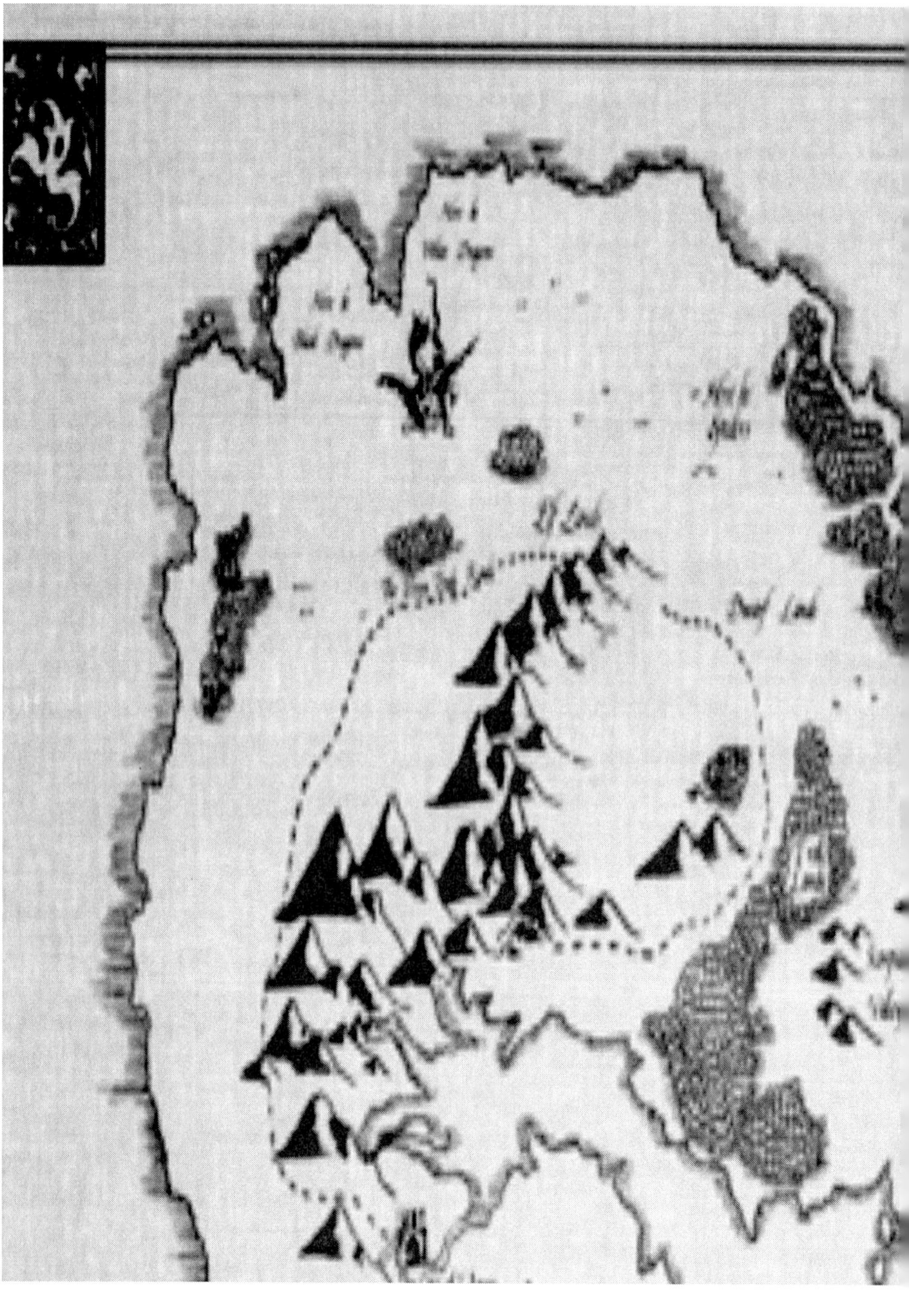

Sophia and the Dragons Books 1 and 2

Many years passed by, Sophia was happy. She went back home every year and John never appeared, so she went back one last time and said good-bye to her home in Europe, and returned forever to Camelot.

36

THE MAN got out of the cab, paid the driver and looked at the house he used to live in. He wondered if anyone was home, it was two stories made of stone. He looked around the grounds, it needed mowing. The place looked deserted, he wondered where everyone was. He didn't want to give anyone a shock when they saw him.

He approached the house and knocked on the door. There was no answer, so he went over to the flowerpot and moved the plant. There was a small hole underneath it with a cover, he pulled on the hook. It was snug, but finally came off; he would have to fix that. He was relieved a key was still there, and pulled it out. He stood up, brushing off the dirt on his knees and put the key into the lock. He heard a click and reached for the knob, turning it to open the door. He stepped inside, it was quiet, no barking or voices, and then he reached for the switch and flipped it. The light came on above him; he looked at the hanging chandelier. It threw a shadow through the hallway. He walked into the kitchen, turning on more lights. He thought it was good the electricity was still on. He saw a strange cell phone sitting on an envelope. He moved the phone and looked at the envelope. It had his name on it; he ripped it open, his heart beating fast. He started reading.

My Dearest,

If you ever return, if it's possible, I was informed all of you were lost and we had a funeral in DC with full colors for all of you. I gave the other widows money for their children's college; I knew it would be harder for them raising their children on their own.

Grandpa is now with us in Cornwall, the only difference is that we are in the year 1190 A.D. of Our Lord. Grandpa is now our Catholic Priest; I run a school along with Jennie, my sister, and Susan. Yes, I found Jennie and Richard. Leila is a young lady now and helps me teach the violin to students. She comes back to Luxembourg quite often to check on the house, pay the electric bill and see if you have been around. Once a year I have made it back too. The last time I left this letter for you, in-case you return, but this will be my last time back. I have waited 10 years, I need to make a commitment and live my life. I will always love you. Kanani is still young acting and has made a friend with a white dragon named Gunther. He is 13 years old and is my friend too. Unbelievable! I would never believe this unless I saw it, but it's the life I'm living. Use this phone if you come home soon. I can't live here; it's become my home. I have Susan, Kimo, Jennie, Richard, Kanani, Gunther, Titus, my new dog, and many others as family. I'm a friend with King Arthur, and many as well. It's been a long time, so I don't really expect a miracle this far down the road. Just know that I have always loved you and prayed for your safe return from the war.

Love Always, Sophia

John dropped the letter and sat down. He had to reread it to comprehend what Sophie had just written. She came over once a year after all these years, 10 to be exact, to leave him a letter, in-case he was alive. Oh, if she only knew what he and the others had lived through. He got up and looked in the fridge, to his surprise there was a bottle of wine in there with a tag saying <u>welcome home John</u>, he decided to take it out and open it. He poured himself a glass after locating the opener, and took it outside to the porch. It was early summer and the sun was just setting. It was too quiet here without Sophie and Kanani. Did he really want to live in Camelot? He was from this time, and he just survived hell. He just couldn't make that decision right now. Perhaps Sophie had remarried since this letter was left. He went back in and picked up the letter again, it was dated January 1, 2023/1190. It was 2024 and June, she hadn't come back this year, and there wasn't a new letter from her. He decided he should call his hotel in Hawaii and see if he still owned it. The only phone was the cell phone on the counter, he picked it up and dialed the number he knew by heart. He got ahold of the front office and they put him through to the manager, it was still Mike, his old friend.

"Hello this is Mike; how can I help

you?"

"Mike, I called to see how the hotel is running, this is John."

There was silence.

"Hold on, John, is this really you? I thought you were killed on that mission ten years ago in Afghanistan! Does Sophie know? Where are you?"

"Ok, take a deep breath Mike. Yes, it's me John, I just walked into the Luxembourg house. No, I have not spoken to Sophie. You're the first person I've talked to."

"Well you know she lives in England now. I've wanted to go visit her, but could never get a hold of her." Mike said. "Maybe you should come here before you go see her and then I can go with you to England to break the news! That sounds like fun." Mike was getting excited.

"Slow down my friend. Let me sleep it on and I'll call you tomorrow." John was getting tired.

"Ok, I'll wait until noon to call you, give me a number."

"Let me look at the phone number." John pulled the phone away from his ear and looked at it. There wasn't a number. "There isn't a number on it. I'll call you when I get up in the morning my friend."

"Ok, John. You get some rest and we'll catch up tomorrow." Then he hung up.

John put the phone down. He had a lot to think about.

He poured himself another glass of wine and went back outside to drink it. The temperature was still warm and the sun had set. It was so nice here, after where he had been all of these years. The world and Sophie thought he was dead, was he too late to go find her? Would it be fair to her? He was thinking it was better for him to maybe live alone. He was a different man now, he had seen so much horror. The camp the men had been drug off to was inhumane for any living creature. Speaking of which, he slapped his knee.

"That's it, I need a dog. If this doesn't work out with Sophie and Kanani I'm getting one." He stood up and went back inside of the house.

He decided to find the guest room and sleep there. It was just too odd to sleep in their room, without Sophie. He got ready for bed and thought for a long while, then sleep overcame him. Something woke him up. He got out of bed and turned on the lamp next to him. He listened, what had awakened him? Was it just a dream? He decided to turn off the light and try to go back to sleep. He tossed and turned then just gave up and jumped into the shower, daylight was just breaking. Afterwards he found keys to the vehicles outside and decided to go into Luxembourg for some breakfast. He drove around the town, things looked different, but they were coming back to him. He decided on a café, so found a parking spot nearby. People were looking at him a bit strangely, maybe it was just his imagination. He sat down at a table and ordered a breakfast of poached eggs, whole wheat toast and sausage, then enjoyed his coffee reading the paper. He was sitting outside in the café and he couldn't help but here the different conversations around him. Then something got his attention and he put his paper down to listen.

"We're going to Camelot in two weeks for a vacation. This is so exciting that we can actually buy tickets for a trip there." the woman said.

"It's about time something like this is possible. I hope you don't like it so much that you will want to move there. We couldn't afford the visa's right now honey." said the man.

The conversation went on and on. What John got from this conversation is that he could buy a ticket for 48 hours, a month's visit, or pay a huge fee and get a visa for a year, then every year come back and renew it. This definitely had the fingerprints of Sophia all over it. He couldn't wait to find her! He paid his bill and drove home, then grabbed the phone and went outside to call Mike in Hawaii. After he hung up, he drove to the airport and booked a flight out that night to Hawaii from Luxembourg.

37

MEANWHILE BIG THINGS were happening in Camelot and in the land of L'Azure, south of Camelot.

There was an evil, selfish, false king in the land of L'Azure, his name was Arden, and this was the most desirable land in the south

Kingdom, because the mountains were filled with unblemished gold. He had stolen the throne by unscrupulous methods. In L'Azure there was a river that dived the land into two parts, the dragons had the unblemished mountains, their land was unmarked with beautiful trees and big caves for the dragons. These dragons were white dragons, the most peaceful and loving of all dragons, like Sophie's Gunther; the men of L'Azure had lived across from them for many centuries and were not afraid of the dragons. Their former King and the dragons had lived in harmony for many many years. The evil King that ruled now ignored all of that, he wanted the gold........

38

KING ARDEN GOT WHATEVER he wanted, all of his life, the people he now ruled were terrified of what he would do. He was not the rightful King, he had seized the throne after coming back from war, his cousin, Agalone and his uncle, King Harlon mysteriously didn't return from war with him. The people didn't know how this could happen, King Harlon was a beloved king, his son Agalone would have been another beloved king. There had been prosperity and peace in the land. They were friends with the dragons, Elves and many others in the land across the water. The King and his wife were very kind, too kind. After all they had adopted the brutal monster that was sitting on the throne; out of compassion for him, when King Harlon's sister had begged them to take him. The King was his uncle, they had taken him in when his father found out that his mother had an affair and bore an illegitimate son, Arden. It had not been easy and Queen Nabila being so kind did not regret taking him in, but she was starting too. Arden was 30 years old now, the Queen had always feared for her children. Arden was greedy and cunningly got whatever he wanted from the King. Her fears started coming to light when her son Agalone and Arden were old enough to go to battle with King Harlon. Queen Nabila had a dream that frightened her before the three of them left for the battle in the Eastern lands. She had begged her husband not to take the young men with him, but to leave them home to protect the town. King Harlon thought it best that his son and his nephew see a real battle with him. Another King from the eastern lands was on his way to invade L'Azure and capture the dragons. King Harlon was sworn to always protect them. He had an agreement with them; he had left for battle about two years ago. The King and Prince Agalone mysteriously didn't return, to the sorrow of the Queen and people of the land. It was rumored that Arden had something to do with their deaths, but Queen Nabila had no proof. Arden wasted no time to be sworn in as the next King. The Queen did not attend his inauguration. She was still in mourning over the loss of her husband and son.

    Queen Nabila and King Harlon had a younger child, a son. Queen Nabila was now thinking of him, thankful she had been so wise to hide him. He would be 20 now, King Harlon and Queen Nabila had made arrangements with the dragons after his birth to hide him with the Elves for safe keeping, he would be the true King one day if anything happened to King Harlon and Prince Abalone. That time was now! She was so thankful that they had thought ahead. She didn't want him to die in some freak accident, she felt in her heart that her oldest son and husband had died at the hands of his cousin Arden.

Back to the story,....

Greed grew in King Arden's heart as he gazed on the pristine land across the river. His desire grew and grew to own that land. King Arden needed money, because he was running out of gold. The war had cost too much and there was not a lot of gold left. Even though he had only been King for a few months, he had changed the kingdom and ruined the land. He made the peasants work very hard to get the remaining gold out of the mountains, but there wasn't enough. He made them slaves to his greed. Evil grew and King Arden decided to take the gold from the dragons. The only problem was that there was a wide, deep river and the land across the way was inhabited with Dragons, Dwarves, Elves, Orgs, Trolls, magic, and who knew what else. King Arden remembered vaguely of another child that was still alive, it started worrying him if he would be challenged for the throne one day. He didn't remember what his name was, but could find out, he didn't know what he looked like, but could guess. So, whether it was the desire for the gold and land he didn't have or the anger and fear of King Harlon and Queen Nabila's son taking the throne from him some day, he planned to take the dragons' land.

One rainy dark morning King Arden called the pheasants from his balcony and made an announcement.

The town people were told that they must build a bridge across the river so that they could harvest the dragons' gold. They would have to get the crusher and slew over the bridge as well to get the gold back to the castle. L'Azure was known to be the richest kingdom in the world and it was about to become bigger and richer. What he didn't tell the people was that L'Azure was broke and they would be starving soon. He had wasted all the money with fine jewels, clothes, anything he wanted. He needed that gold and land!

The dragons had attended the funeral for King Harlon and Prince Agalone, they had no bodies, but there was a ceremony. There was reason to find the Prince because Agalone is the rightful King, the false King must be taken out, Queen Nabila had talked to Teyrnon about getting her other son.

"Teyrnon, we will need to find our son that was hidden with the Elves. Have you any word of him?"

"Your Majesty, we have kept an eye on him. He has grown into a fine young man, he has been taught by Meuric the Wizard. Prince Eamon knows swordsmanship, he has humility, leadership, and most of all he has love and compassion for others. He will make a great leader someday, however, he doesn't know that he is the rightful King." Teyrnon hesitated, "Should we get him?"

Queen Nabila's eyes narrowed as she searched for Arden, "Yes, we need to find him and bring him home. I fear Arden will not give up the throne easily, the sooner the better. How long will it take to get him?"

"It will take a long time, it's a very treacherous and long journey through the mountains to Elf land, when I get home, I will arrange a group of courageous dragons to come with me on that journey."

£

Thinking back on this conversation, Queen Nabila had been right to fear Arden. They couldn't find Prince Eamon in the time they had before Arden seized the throne, but they would do it before he ruined anymore lives, they had to find him; Arden had already ruined the Kingdom that King Harlon and Queen Nabila had made. The land was looking desecrated.

A few days had passed, Teyrnon was trying to get word to Meuric the Wizard and Emmorous had been keeping an eye on the Kingdom from the dragons' side for some time now. One evening Emmorous saw something that frightened him more than anything ever had. He immediately started searching for Teyrnon.

"Teyrnon look!" Emmorous the dragon was upset as he barged into Teyrnon's cave.

"What is it Emmorous?" Teyrnon looked up and then took off his glasses and placed them on his shelf. He stood up and followed Emmorous out of his enormous, clean cave. Teyrnon followed Emmorous to the high banks of the River Elwha and saw what had gotten his fellow dragon so upset.

"This is bad, we must have a meeting at once. Hurry get the others, we must meet in our community cave and talk about this at once!"

Teyrnon turned to go back to his cave and got the map of the land, while Emmorous trotted off as fast as a dragon can, to get the other dragons alerted.

Teyrnon knew the evil thoughts in the minds of some evil men and King Arden was one of those. He knew they were coming to destroy their land, just as he had destroyed the land that did not rightly belong to him. The dragons were not greedy, and didn't need gold for anything, but Teyrnon had an idea to save the land.

The cave was full of dragons talking when Teyrnon entered. He took his place in the front of the group. Teyrnon cleared his voice, "HMMM......" until he got their attention.

"It has been brought to our attention that we are in imminent danger from men. This is our land, it was given to us many many centuries past by our elders who gave it to us. We must send a party of dragons to get the black and white dragons, the Dwarves, Elves and Wizards to come to our aid, warn them of our danger.

Along the way we must find Prince Eamon and bring him back, he is the true leader of the land. We must help him take the throne. For, if men like Arden take our land, they will eventually take everyone's land as well. We must have three of the youngest, strongest, and bravest dragons go on this journey, then we must have guards on the banks to keep an eye on the men. Do I have volunteers?" Teyrnon looked around, he was pleased to see so many volunteering.

"I want to go," Albe stepped forward.

"Me too," Aedan joined him.

"Count me in," Machel said and then looked down at his little brother, Cham.

Teyrnon also looked at Machel's little brother. "Cham, you are old enough to go if you listen to the others, but I really could use you on the bank making sure we keep the men from crossing."

Cham's eyes grew large, "That would be an honor to be able to stay and have that duty!

Thank you, sir!"

Teyrnon chuckled, "Great, it's settled then, why don't the three of you stay behind and Emmorous will get you ready for your trip. As for the others, I will get the crew that is going to be on guard duty, we can meet outside. The rest of you will have to do the chores and feed the watch crew. Hopefully, this won't go on for too long, but we have to prepare in case it does." Teyrnon walked out of the cave and walked over to the bank, ten dragons followed him.

"Cham, I'm going to assign you as crew chief. You have the responsibility of running to get help, if help is needed." Teyrnon looked around, "Arthur, you oversee how many dragons you think we need out here, and who is here in rotating shifts."

Cham's whole dragon face light up with delight that he would have this responsibility.

Arthur stepped forward, "I will be honored sir to have this duty." He looked around and started talking to the dragons. Then he turned to

Teyrnon, "Is it ok with you that we melt the structure daily?"

"Ha ha, what an excellent plan that is...." Teyrnon chuckled. "It will really make the King angry, we must be ready for him to retaliate."

"We will be ready, sir." Egon stood tall, he was a young dragon, still a teenager. The older dragons had stayed in the old land and had given the younger dragons this land to keep everyone safe from invasion. It was a smart thing to do, because the time had now come. Everyone in the land would be aware of this soon and together they would ban together and be safe. They must prepare housing for the Elves, Dwarves and Wizards.

It was getting dark and the men on the shore were packing up their bags to go home to their wives and families for dinner. This was the time for the dragons to get to work. By midnight the dragons had undone everything the men had accomplished. It was tiring work, so a new shift of dragons would stay hidden watching the men in the morning. There would be shock and anger to be sure, not from the men, but the King.

The three dragons were to take off at the break of day for their long journey into the lands of their ancestors. Hopefully, there was still peace, and no one was at war with one another. Hopefully they could bring the Prince back to rule the land and be one again.

Teyrnon was thinking how smart it was for the baby Prince to have been hidden safely away from the evil that prevailed in the Kingdom of men.

"If only I could get ahold of Meuric the Wizard!" Teyrnon muttered to himself as he went back to his cave.

In the middle of the night there was some commotion outside, Teyrnon hurried out.

"What is going on?" He asked Egan, looking around. Then before he got an answer he saw what it was!

39

SEVERAL SMALL BOATS were crossing way down the river. Teyrnon and the others hurried to see who it was. Then to their surprise, they recognized the Queen, some maids, and guards. Things must be bad. The Queen called out to Teyrnon.

"Teyrnon, can you help us? We need to take refuge with you." She was helped out of the boat by one of her men.

"My Lady, we will have to find accommodations for you." Teyrnon was a bit worried.

"We brought tents, Teyrnon, but we must be far enough back from the water, where the bridge is being built. I feared for my life in my own castle! Arden killed John and then Agalone, I have proof now. I was such a fool, but I won't be again. Have you gone to find my son yet?" Queen Nabila looked up at Teyrnon.

She was still beautiful even though her face was full of sorrow. Her golden silver hair was braided, she had on a casual red dress and was very graceful. Teyrnon wondered how something so bad could be happening to the Kingdom and the Queen right now, then answered her.

"We are sending three dragons tomorrow to find him and bring help." Teyrnon led the way for all of them to follow as they talked.

"I want to go with them." Queen Nabila said breathless trying to keep up with Teyrnon's pace.

"My Lady, it will be a rough trip." Teyrnon

stopped and turned around to talk to her, he tried to convince her it was a bad idea. "Why don't you get set up in your tents and we will talk."

"Yes, good." She asked her guards to set the tents by the side of Teyrnon's cave. "Is that a good place Teyrnon?"

"It is, now let me get the map and we can sit by the fire, I will bring the three dragons going on the journey over to meet you as well."

"Splendid." Queen Nabila gave Teyrnon a warm smile.

A little while later, the tents were set up, food was being cooked. It was in the middle of the night, but the Queen and her people had not had time for dinner. Teyrnon had to wake the young dragons from a deep sleep and give them the news that the Queen was among them now. Machel, Albe and Aedan were honored and excited to meet Queen Nabila, so they hurried after Teyrnon.

Emmorous, Machel, Albe, Aedan, Teyrnon, Queen Nabila and her head guard, George gathered around the open fire George's men had made. Queen Nabila had only brought one of her maids to help her, she had sent the others away to good families and to hide from the wicked King.

Teyrnon put the map on a table and showed George the path they were going to follow.

"After leaving here, the dragons will go around the back side of our caves, then they will enter a large forest, which leads to the first village of Dwarves. There they will stay one night, more if needed and enlist the Dwarves help. The Dwarves can then assemble and come back here to help us. We need all of the help we can get, because it is a long journey to the Elves and Wizards. From there the trip will continue to the other shore on the far side of this island, where the Black Dragons now live near the White Dragons." Teyrnon stopped and looked to see what the Queen had to say.

"I still want to go, Anna, my maid and George too. The other guards will stay here to help protect this land." Queen Nabila stood up. "I need some sleep, we need provisions for such a journey too."

"If you insist on going my Queen, then I have no choice but to also go. You will travel with your maid on my back. George can ride one of the other dragons, I believe Machel is big enough to carry him." Teyrnon looked at Machel, Machel nodded yes. "Perhaps this is better anyway, when we find the Prince, it will be his mother that greets him. We will leave tomorrow afternoon, this will give us enough time to get ready. Good night my Lady Nabila, Anna, and George; come along Emmorous, Machel, Albe, and Aedan. Emmorous, you will be in charge here until I return." As they walked off, Teyrnon and Emmorous made plans. It would be daylight soon and the journey would be long and dangerous. It was dangerous to be here as well, danger was everywhere!

40

THE NEXT MORNING there was noise coming from the other side of the river. The men showed up for work and saw that all the work they had done was destroyed. The King showed up and started yelling at the men to rebuild, then he looked over at the dragons' caves and started yelling threats at the them as well.

Teyrnon listened and chuckled, thinking out loud he said, "Wait until they find the Queen has escaped with her people! I think we had better get everyone up and start our journey."

Teyrnon looked behind him as he left his cave, "I have everything I need." Then left to find the Queen already with Emmorous, talking to him about what to do if the King should become bothersome while she was away.

£

The King was furious! After leaving the river he marched into the Castle bellowing for Queen Nabila to come to him at once. He kept looking up from his breakfast to see if she was approaching yet. Finally, he slammed his fork down onto his plate and stormed off to her chambers.

He approached her suite and stopped, "This is odd! Where is her guard and where are her ladies in waiting?" He got an awful feeling in his gut as he swung open the double doors. He looked around. There wasn't anyone to be seen, he walked over to her dressing table and looked, her brushes were gone! He threw open her wardrobe to see that is was virtually empty! He turned around and looked everything over. "She has gone for her son! I must find her!" Then he stormed out and called for his guards.

£

"My Lady, I see you are up and ready very early this morning. How did you rest?" Teyrnon asked the Queen.

"Good morning Teyrnon, I slept better than I have in years last night. I'm anxious to get on our way before Arden knows I am here and tries to stop me." Queen Nabila was looking at Teyrnon.

"I agree, he must know that you have left the palace by now. Come, let us get the dragons over to your camp, they are packed and ready to go." Teyrnon called the dragons going on the trip to follow the Queen, they hurried over, greeted everyone and started towards the camp.

As they arrived at the camp there was a sudden on slot of activity from the other side. The King was approaching on horseback followed by some soldiers. He rode the edge of the bank and shouted out, "I'm coming to get you Queen Nabila!" Then he turned around and rode out of town, with his men close behind him.

Teyrnon heard Arden's words and turned to talk to the Queen, her people and his dragons.

"It will take them two days to ride down the Peninsula to the piece of land that allows them to cross over. We will be long gone in the other direction by then. I will have my dragons waiting for him and discourage his crossing. If he starts shooting at them, they will have no choice but to fight back. It is not in our blood to fight as white dragons, but we will defend our land and everyone living in it. We must take off now."

The guard, George said, "Thank you for

that reassurance Teyrnon, we must get to the Dwarves, so they can come assist your dragons and my men."

"You are very welcome, now I will crouch down, please help the ladies onto my back." Teyrnon did as he said, when Queen Nabila and Anna were securely in place, Teyrnon stood up.

George climbed onto Machel. Then the dragons walked out of camp and took flight.

"Hang on!" Teyrnon called out to the women.

"This is magnificent! I love it!" Queen Nabila shouted laughing.

Teyrnon heard her and chuckled, but he had to continue paying attention to where he was flying.

Anna was enjoying herself as well, but she was a little bit more frightened than the Queen.

Teyrnon and the others turned and flew over the cliffs of Moher, this was on the opposite side of the island away from the water that separated the Castle and the dragons.

Queen Nabila gasped, "Oh, this is beautiful!"

"Yes, it is," Teyrnon replied.

They followed this coastline for many miles then crossed the water and turned in towards the looming forest. They landed just before the forest got thick.

"I think we should stop here and take a rest, we will need to go into the forest to meet the Dwarves, but there are nasty Trolls we will need to avoid." Teyrnon warned everyone.

George slid off Machel's back, I will start a fire and we can have a bite to eat." He looked up at the sky, "it's late afternoon, do you think we should try entering the forest today or wait until the first thing in the morning, Teyrnon?"

Teyrnon looked at the young dragons, he knew they were exhausted from that long flight they just took. "I think perhaps we should find a place and set up camp for the night, George."

"Thank you, Teyrnon, Albe, Aedan and I are beat." Machel spoke for all of them. The others shook their heads in agreement.

"I thought so," Teyrnon said, "why don't you get us something to eat and we can have a good rest here. Besides, Trolls come out at night. We need to find cover for everyone to sleep." Teyrnon looked around and found a cave. "Why don't you go have a look at that Cave, Machel; Albe and Aedan, why don't you get us some food. I'll get some wood and help George make a fire. They will then be able to cook their dinner and we can ward off the Trolls if there are any."

£

The Elves were holding a meeting, Meuric the Wizard had just arrived with news.

"I'm sorry to have to bring this news, it

has come to my attention that the young princes' father has been killed in battle, then his older brother murdered, he is the rightful heir to the throne. An interloper, his cousin, has taken the throne. He has destroyed the land in the little time he has been in power, he has made the people of the land slaves to do his work. The Queen and the Dragons are coming to find him. Threwien you have raised him as your own, would you like to talk to Eamon, or shall I?" Meuric waited for an answer.

"I want us both to be there, I will explain what I know and then you can answer the questions I do not know. Let us do this now." Threwien stood up and excused himself from the meeting. Meuric followed Threwien to his dwelling.

Prince Eamon was outside practicing bowing, when he saw his dad and Meuric coming he threw down his bow and ran over to greet them.

"What a pleasure to see both of you, how

was the meeting?" Prince Eamon asked.

"Fine son, come with us, we have a story to tell you." Threwien motioned for Eamon to follow them to the stream. Threwien sat down on a tree log, Meuric stood looking at the flowing water and Eamon sat down next to his dad. Curiosity was eating him up, what was up? He didn't know, but knew it was big.

"A long time ago, there was a kingdom that was full of love and beauty. It is land very far from here, it's full of men, like you Eamon." Eamon started to say something, but Threwien put up his hand to stop him. "Let me finish, then you can ask as many questions as you wish." Eamon shook his head in understanding.

"This land had a beautiful Queen that the people adored, her husband was the King that men followed into battle without a blink or question that it was the right thing to do. There was plenty of food, the town was flourishing in gold production. They had a peaceful agreement with the dragons that lived across from them and all of the people in the land. In fact, King Harlon and Queen Nabila were great friends of the Elves. I knew them very well. They were too kind and took in a nephew of King Harlon to raise as their own. He was an evil kid and they feared for their youngest son. They had another son, ten years older than this son, but the baby they hid away. It was a good thing they did too, for the time has come for the Queen to come get her son." Threwien took a moment and looked at Eamon, there was understanding in his eyes.

"That son, is me?" Eamon asked.

"Yes, it is, your father was murdered and your brother too, by your cousin. His name is Arden and he has taken the throne. All of us are here to help you and your mother retake the kingdom and make it a good place again. Arden has made the people slaves, he has taken all of the gold and now wants the dragons' land. We have a pact with the dragons and men to always take care of one another. I will always be in your life, Eamon, ummmm, Prince Eamon it is." Threwien hugged Eamon.

"This is more than I can take in right now. When are the dragons and Queen, my mother, coming?" Eamon asked.

"Soon, they left L'Azure last night, they should be in troll country tonight. We are getting an army of Elves together to go back with you." Threwien stood up and looked at Meuric.

"Do you have any questions Eamon? I will always be with you, I'm the one that brought you here to hide. These elves have done an excellent job of doing just that, they have raised a holy, humble, hard-working, young prince." Meuric finished, Eamon stood and put his arms around the elf and the wizard.

There was going to be hard times ahead and his whole life had changed, all of his friends he had grown up with, how was he going to tell them?

"I must say good bye to my friends and get things in order, Father and Meuric." Eamon said as they left the stream.

"I'm sure your friends have already heard from their fathers about you. Go see them, we must get ready for our journey into the L'Azure Kingdom." Threwien patted his adopted son on the back, he was proud of Eamon and would miss the boy. Threwien choked back tears as he watched Eamon walk away.

£

It was just past midnight and George was dozing by the fire, Teyrnon was sleeping next to him, when there was a crash!

41

TEYRNONE ROARED and spit out fire! A troll was burned and started running away. George went to find the women and warn them of the troll attack. The other dragons gathered around Teyrnon and peered into the woods. Teyrnon knew that at daybreak they need to get out of here, more trolls gathered around the one that caught on fire, and started shooting arrows at the dragons. The dragons guarded the cave and spit out more fire, then Teyrnon took off into the air and breathed fire on the forest. Pretty soon the trolls were running out of the forest and away from the caves. The other dragons took off after them. The nasty trolls were a nuisance, always had been. They terrorized the dragons, Dwarves and men of this land. Tonight, was long in coming.

The trolls started shooting fire arrows at the flying dragons, Teyrnon looked at the others and they knew what that meant. Pretty soon the trolls would crawled under big rocks to protect themselves. They had to hide in daylight or they turned into stone, so the dragons flew back to the caves. George and the women had food ready and were packed to go.

"Is everyone ok?" George asked.

"Yes, a few scratches from the arrows, but nothing life threatening. We need to eat fast and leave. We have more territory with unfriendly residents to cross, before we get to the Dwarves."

Teyrnon grabbed a bite and looked around. "The next territory is water and we have water trolls to deal with."

"Oh no, this is very scary." Queen Nabila looked around to make sure no trolls were watching them.

"Yes, it is, but we will make it." Teyrnon tried to assure her.

£

Back in the land of L'Azure, King Arden was furious! The Queen had taken off with the dragons to some faraway place! The dragons had kept him from following the Queen. He rode back to his kingdom and called his men together. They had to stop the Queen from finding her son, there was another way around without going past the dragons, it was a lot longer, but the only way. He had the men get fresh horses and food prepared. They would take off at first light, they would have to ride around the sides of the island and go into the mountains around the other side. He was unaware of the trolls lurking or hostile dragons he would have to deal with. His blind rage and fear drove him to hunt down the Queen and kill her.

42

IN ANOTHER KINGDOM, Gunther, Sophie's Dragon, approached Sophie one cold morning in Camelot. She heard him outside and opened her front door.

"Why Gunther, you look worried, what is it?" Sophie stepped outside.

"My cousin Teyrnon is in trouble. There has been unrest in the land of L'Azure, he is on a journey to find the lost prince." Gunther was giving Sophie that look she knew only too well.

"What must we do?" she asked.

"We must get some dragons and men to go help hold down the village until others come to help, and the prince is found." Gunther answered.

"I heard about some kind of uprising, how the King and his son were killed. I wonder what King Arthur knows about this? Let me go talk to Lamorak and see what is known. I will get back to you Gunther." Sophie turned and called her dogs, Kanani and Titus.

Gunther thanked her and went back to his cave to wait for her answer.

Kanani trotted after Sophie, and Titus trotted after Kanani, Sophie was in search of her knight. She decided to go to her sister, Jennie, and ask if her husband, Richard, knew anything first. Sophie knocked on her sister's door, just a few houses down from Sophie's.

Jennie opened her door, "Hi sis, come in. Hi Kanani, hi Titus!"

Kanani wagged her tail, Titus tilted her head and looked at Jenni. It was a German Shepherd thing that made Sophie and Jennie laugh.

Jennie is Sophie's older sister, Jennie is 5 feet, 6 inches, slender with dark hair, she has one daughter, Leila. Sophie raised Leila, when Jennie and her husband Richard went missing on an expedition in Egypt. They both met each other again in Camelot.

"Hi Jennie," Sophie kissed her on the cheek. "I have a question. Gunther has asked me to find out what I know about the changes in the land of L'Azure. I thought maybe Richard might know something. Could you ask him for me?"

"You can ask him yourself, he's in the other room." Jennie got up and a opened a door, sticking her head inside. "Richard, could you spare a moment for Sophie, love?"

Richard looked up from his writing, "Of course, funny she should come over this morning." Richard stood up and walked over to the door kissing Jennie.

"Why is it funny?" Jennie asked.

"Well, Lamorak has me going over some battle strategies, there seems to be some unrest in the land of L'Azure, and we are not sure if we should intervene or not." Richard turned to greet Sophie.

"Hi Sophie," he kissed her on top of her head. Richard was 6 feet tall, dark hair, muscular, and handsome, Sophie was 5 feet, 4 inches, long blond hair and very slender in her blue cotton dress and sandals.

"Well, I guess you do know something about the land of L'Azure, I heard you talking to Jennie. Gunther has asked me to find out some information. He thinks we should go help them, his cousin is on a quest to find the missing prince to take over the throne, and usurp the false king." Sophie sat back down.

Richard pulled up a stool to the table. He started drawing out what he knew on a slate. "See here, this is L'Azure, it is a kingdom to our southwest, we would have to go by water to get there. The king and queen's nephew have taken the throne. It is believed he was responsible for his uncle and cousin's deaths to get the throne. The kingdom is in ruins, the people are slaves and have revolted now that their queen has left to find the true heir to the throne. We are not sure King Arthur will take a direct role in this, he may let us go on a quest though, to help." Richard looked up at the women.

"That is all I need to know, let me go find Lamorak." Sophie stood up.

"I will go with you, I need to show him what I have found and the plans I have drawn up. Let me get them from the study and I'll be right out." Richard left the room.

Jennie took Sophie's hands in hers. "If Richard goes, we must go too."

"Yes, I agree. I know Lamorak will say no

though." Sophie whispered.

"He he, so will Richard, but we have the dragons to take us." Jennie giggled.

Sophie giggled too, Richard came out and caught them in their little conspiracy.

"I'm ready, now you ladies are not going to plot anything are you?" Richard asked.

Sophie looked like she didn't know what he was talking about, letting go of her sister's hand.

"Now, dear, we are planning no such thing. Run along, oh, actually, I need to go out. May I join you? Jennie asked sweetly.

"Yes, get your jacket." Richard smiled.

The three of them, Titus, and Kanani, the German Shepherds, left the house in search of Lamorak, Sophie's knight.

Someday he would be her knight, if she would just marry him, Kanani thought, as she trotted along beside Sophie.

They found Lamorak as he was on his horse riding in the direction of Sophie's house. He pulled up alongside of Sophie and jumped down off his horse.

"I was just coming to get you my Lady, Sophie." Lamorak leaned over, took her hand and kissed it.

"I was on my way to find you, but stopped at Jennie and Richard's first." Sophie laughed.

"Well, please tell me what is on your mind." Lamorak looked into her eyes.

Before Sophie answered, Richard spoke up. "Lamorak, Sophie is asking about the land of L'Azure's uprising. Gunther has approached her, here are the plans I came up with. It is my opinion, that should King Arthur not get involved directly, that he will let us go on a quest. Is this a possibility?"

Taking the plans, Lamorak took a quick look and answered, "Yes, it is, I just left him. That was why I was coming to find you Sophie, to tell you that I am leaving with Richard and some knights to go on a quest to help protect the dragons land, the elves and everyone else that is being threatened by the false king. We need to help the rightful heir take back the throne in L'Azure. King Arthur wants a full report and is giving us the majority of the knights from the Round Table, he needs to keep a few to protect this kingdom." Lamorak looked at Sophie, she had a frown on her forehead.

"Gunther wants to go, if he goes, I go." Sophie stated firmly.

"Oh, my dear, it does not go that way, it is far too dangerous. I will not put you in harms way my love." He put his arm around her and kissed her.

Jennie gave Sophie a look. "Ok, well, I tried. When do you leave?" Sophie asked Lamorak.

"In the morning, we have the big party tonight, Sophie." Lamorak looked like he was going to kiss Sophie, but he just grinned, "I will come for you around 5. In the meantime, I have much to prepare. Richard could you come with me? We soon have a meeting with the other knights." Lamorak jumped back on his horse.

"Yes, I will walk beside you." Richard looked back at Jennie, "I will be home in time to get ready for the party, you get ready too."

Jennie waved him goodbye.

Both men were too busy talking to notice what the women were up too.

Sophie looked at Jennie, "Let's go find Gunther." Jennie nodded in agreement, both of them took off to find the dragon.

Arriving at the caves, Sophie called Gunther. He came out and Sophie told him what was going on.

"Great, Jennie and I need to pack lightly, we will be here after the men leave in the morning, Gunther. What other dragons are going?" Sophie asked.

Gunther named Drake and some of the other dragons too.

"Sophie, I have a feeling that this is the night that Lamorak is going to ask you for your hand in marriage. He's waited ten years, you told him ten years you had to wait to marry. John has not returned, so tonight if he asks you, say yes when he asks. That poor man has waited so long for you to marry him. He loves you so much, the two of you are such a great couple when you're together." Jennie was giving Sophie a big sisterly talk.

"I know, I know." Said Sophie, "I'm putting on my blue dress that he loves so much. Kanani and baby Titus have had their baths, I want them clean and looking nice tonight too. We are going to have such a fun time at the party King Arthur is giving us in the castle. Even Gunther and the dragons will be there! "Well, I need to clean up for my date tonight Jennie. I've got butterflies in my stomach. I know that after all of this time, I'm not making a mistake, if he asks me again." Sophie put her arm through Jennie's arm and they walked back home together making plans.

After leaving Jennie, Sophia left to get ready, more emotionally than physically. She still had her long blond hair, she had kept her weight down. Well, really, they were eating so much healthier here than back in her time. Everything was from the earth, a lot of root vegetables and good wine. She had already fed the dogs but knew they would get some scraps tonight too. Everyone loved Kanani and adorned little Titus, they led pretty good lives. By the day they played in the lake with Gunther and the other dragons, then ran through Camelot. They were in her classroom when she was teaching, they went everywhere with her and they loved Lamorak, he felt the same way too. She was so excited! She had waited over ten years to remarry, It's actually been eleven years since John's death, Sophia thought. Sophie was in her late 20's, so she was still young. She was going to tell Kanani and baby Titus to stay home, but changed her mind when she saw their faces looking at her all dressed up.

"Ok, you two can go, but behave yourselves, no jumping up and stealing food off people's plates Titus."

I won't Sophie, Titus wagged his tail at her. Sophie had to laugh; they brought her so much delight. There was a knock on her door, Sophia went over to answer it and to her surprise, it was Lamorak already!

"Hi Sophie," he said, "I've come to escort you to the party tonight. I see the pups are ready to go too. Good thing I brought my carriage and not just my horse."

"Hi Lamorak, good thing you didn't, let me get a wrap, you can get the fur kids into the carriage and I'll be right out."

"Ok, kids." Lamorak called the dogs, they ran past him and jumped into the back part of the carriage. By the time Sophia had come out they had settled down, but to her surprise, Gunther was there.

43

TEYRNON, SCOPED the landscape below him. He was looking for water trolls, it was now early morning, so all trolls should be in hiding. The blue water below and the vast landscape surrounding the area was more beautiful than Queen Nabila could ever have imagined. San immense sense of peace, she had lost so many loved ones, her people were in trouble too. She wondered if any of the other Kings in other Kingdoms would hear of her plight and come to her aid. She sighed, it was just a wishful dream.

44

THE KING'S KNIGHTS were preparing their quest, Sophie and Jennie couldn't wait for them to leave so they could take off on the dragons. The knights were going into the kingdom, Gunther was taking Sophie and Jennie to find Teyrnon and give him a hand. However, that very afternoon Leila, Jennie's twenty-year-old daughter arrived at Jennie's house.

"You're back from Luxembourg, Leila!" Jennie kissed her daughter.

"Yes, no sign of John, I don't think he is ever coming back. Sophie should marry Lamorak, mom." Leila sighed.

"Yes, you can mention that to her when we see her in the morning. We are leaving on the dragons for the land of L'Azure in the morning, would you like to come with us? Your father is going with the knights and does not know we are going. Don't mention anything to him at dinner this evening. When he leaves I will fill you in." Leila took her daughter's hand and squeezed it with affection.

Leila laughed, "Mom, you and Sophie are so funny, yes, yes, yes! I want an adventure, I'll go!"

"Hurry, get dressed, there is a big party in the castle tonight." Jennie turned around, "You'd better hurry, dad's just coming in the door."

Richard was delighted to see his daughter, he filled them in with the plans the knights had made, as he was changing to some fine clothing for the party.

"I will miss the two of you very much, take care of one another. I will return as soon as I can. I hope we can save L'Azure's kingdom." Richard stood up, I'm ready, let me escort the two prettiest ladies in Camelot to dinner." He put out an arm for each of them and they left the cottage for some fun.

45

TEYRNON, SAW that the younger dragons were tiring. "Over there," he shouted, "Trees, away from the water. It's still early we can fish and have a rest there." Teyrnon started flying lower to get a better look, he couldn't see any trolls, so he landed by some trees. The men fished, Teyrnon surveyed the area to make sure no one was approaching them. Teyrnon was sure there were Dwarves nearby that could come to their aid. He walked over and approached the Queen's guard, George.

"The Dwarves are nearby, are they not?" Teyrnon asked George.

"I believe so, I remember they took up the mining of gold years ago and were shipping it to us in the town. Then that stopped, so I'm not sure if they moved on or are still here." George looked around. "I must see that Queen Nabila is comfortable, excuse me." George walked off.

Machel, the young dragon approached Teyrnon, "I would like permission to explore the area, to make sure there are no signs of Trolls, maybe find out if anyone else lives here, like the Dwarves?"

"Great idea, no more than a quick flight around the area and then back here." Teyrnon directed him. "Take Aedan or one of the other dragons with you." Teyrnon looked thoughtful. If there are Dwarves, we could perhaps get their help in finding the Prince.

"I will report to you as soon as we return, thank you." Machel took off to find Aedan.

46

"HI GUNTHER, are you going with us to the party?" Sophie asked.

"Yes, I wouldn't miss tonight's party for anything Sophie," Gunther said.

"I'm glad to hear that Gunther," she

laughed.

Lamorak helped Sophia up into the front; she needed it as her dress kept getting in the way.

"Ok, off we go then, it's going to be some party. Sophie and I are going to have a wonderful evening." Lamorak told Gunther.

He grinned at Sophie and she blushed, adjusting her wrap and placing it around her shoulders.

When they got to the palace, Lamorak helped Sophie out, she waited for him with the dogs while he parked the carriage. She looked around, no sign of her sister yet. People were arriving by the dozens now, she had never been to a party like this before, what was the occasion? Sophie wondered, Lamorak had asked for her hand in marriage before and didn't go to all this trouble, so it must be something else. She smiled, Lamorak just showed up. He put out his arm for her and escorted her into the grand hall. She looked around, it was decorated with balloons, flowers, on their table; all of the tables were decked out! Violin music was playing, there was a dance area too. Lamorak found their table, her sister Jennie and husband Richard were to sit with them. They came in a few minutes after Sophie and Lamorak were toasting their first glass of wine.

"Oh my gosh! Leila! You made it back in time." Sophie stood and hugged her niece.

Sophie had practically raised Leila, her sister, Jennie and husband Richard, had taken off on an expedition and never returned, so Leila stayed with her in Hawaii and Luxembourg. After Sophie fell through time, she met them here in Camelot, to her delight and surprise. That was many years later though. Leila had turned into a beautiful young lady at the age of 18.

"Yes, Auntie, I just got back from Luxembourg. I went out with friends, then stopped by the house and grabbed my bag, then hurried back here." Leila sat down in-between Sophie and Jennie.

"You didn't see," Sophie looked at Lamorak, he was talking to Richard, she whispered, "any signs of John, did you?"

"No, I didn't. I don't' think he is coming back, Auntie. We have a great life here though, don't we?" Leila tried to sound convincing.

"Absolutely, we have a GREAT life here." Sophie smiled.

"Lamorak turned around, "How's my girl? Where are our fur kids?" Lamorak looked under the table and saw Kanani and Titus. "Good, everyone is being good, oh, the King and Queen are entering."

Everyone stood up and cheered.

Dinner was served, more wine was served, then Lamorak took Sophie's hand and asked her to dance with him. That's when it happened!

47

LAMORAK LOOKED at the violin players and made a jester. They started playing the most romantic music. Sophie was oblivious until Lamorak twirled her around then grabbed her and knelt in front of her. Sophie held her breathe.

"Sophia Stradivarius Anderson, I have loved you since the first time I saw you on the side of the road with Kanani landing on top of you. There is nothing you could ever do to make me not love you, I will love you with my last breath on earth. You are perfect in every way, there will never be anyone else. Will you finally marry me?"

Everyone was holding their breath, Jennie was crying and Richard had tears in his eyes as well.

"Lamorak, you were the Knight in Shining Armor I have waited my whole life for. You were such a surprise for me. For 10 years you have never let me down, you have been kind and waited for me. YES, I will MARRY YOU!"

Lamorak stood up and placed a diamond ring on Sophie's finger, then gave her a long kiss. Everyone cheered! Jennie came running over hugging Jennie and then Lamorak, she took Sophie's hand and looked at her beautiful ring. Richard and Leila were right behind Jennie, congratulating the couple.

The Knights and the King and Queen both congratulated them as well. It was a grand event, and ended all too soon. The men were leaving early the next morning to go help the people of L'Azure, they needed rest.

That night when Lamorak took Sophie home, he just held her and kissed her softly once more, he had trouble leaving her.

"Honey, I'm going to miss you every minute I'm gone. I can't wait to get back, because that is when we should be married. Do you agree?" Lamorak asked Sophie.

"Yes, let's marry upon your return. There is no reason to wait any longer. Be safe and come home to me in one piece." She kissed him again.

"Ok, I will come see you in the morning before you leave. Good night my love." Sophie opened her door, let the dogs in and slipped through the crack, she didn't look back, because if she did, she wouldn't let him leave. She listened and heard the carriage taking off, then went in to her room and got undressed; after slipping on her nightgown and crawling into bed, she held up her hand and looked at her ring. It was unbelievable that she was marrying a man from another century.

48

THE NEXT MORNING, very early, Sophie, Titus and Kanani got up and went to the castle. Lamorak was waiting for her, his face lit up when he saw her approaching. The knights all cheered again, they were delighted for both of them. Sophie blushed as she put her arms around Lamorak and gave him an endearing kiss. She was going to miss him terribly, she kind of felt bad not telling him she was going to be there, in L'Azure too. He would understand, maybe? Sophie didn't want to start the marriage with a lie so, Sophie decided to tell him.

"Lamorak, darling, there is something I need to tell you." Sophie looked serious.

"Yes?" Lamorak looked at her seriously.

"It's nothing about the engagement." She giggled, it's about having Gunther taking Jennie and me to help find the Prince. We won't be in the fighting, we will be safer than you. I have to help." Sophie saw the relief in his face.

"Sophie, if it's that important to you, I'm not going to say no. Just be safe, I don't want anything happening to you, because when I return, we are getting married." Lamorak hugged her. "You could just stay and plan the wedding?" He asked pleadingly and grinned, but knew she would not do that. "I'm glad you told me, that you trusted me enough to tell me. Jennie needs to tell Richard."

"I'll have her do that right now. I'll be right back." Sophie turned to leave, but Lamorak gently grabbed her arm and pulled her back to him. He gave her a long kiss, then let her go.

Jennie, we are getting ready to leave. I love you Sophie." Lamorak hugged her one more time, then Sophie stepped away running over to her sister.

Jennie congratulated Sophie on her engagement again, then agreed, if she had told Lamorak, it was ok to tell Richard. So, she did and he was happy and relieved that Jennie had told him, and that Gunther was going to help them find the Prince. Jennie was sure he knew of her plans anyway. That meant they would all be home sooner, for the big wedding.

49

MACHEL FLEW DOWN and landed by the queen. "The Dwarfs are nearby!!! I spotted them, we just have to get through this forest and they are in the next forest over. A word of warning about the forest we are in, it looks like big, big, bugs of some kind are gathering, I think we need to load up and move on."

"What kind of big bugs?" asked George.

"I don't know, I have never seen them, they are long, looks like they have pinchers on their front end. They are as big as a human child!" Machel's eyes got big, then Aedan flew down next to Machel.

"Did you see those things???" He gasped and added, "They are headed this way!"

"That's it." Queen Nabila stood up and shuddered, "Let's pack and go." She grabbed her belongings and stuffed them back into her bag. Anna picked up the food, the dragons looked out into the forest, the trees were bending and there was a lot of loud crunching sounds.

"Hurry!" Teyrnon bent down for the women to climb up. The other dragons did the same. They had just taken flight and they saw the things coming out of the forest!

"Those are scorpions!" Queen Nabila screamed and held on tighter to Teyrnon.

"They could have killed us!" Anna cried holding on to the queen.

The Queen started slipping, Teyrnon slowed down, Anna grabbed her, but Queen Nabila's coat was caught on one of Teyrnon's scales. The queen climbed back up and let her other arm out of the jacket. It flew to the ground and was grabbed by the scorpions. They devoured it in minutes. The queen broke down into sobs.

"We are flying out of here, don't worry!" Teyrnon went up a bit higher so the humans couldn't watch the ground so closely.

They flew for about an hour, they were hopefully out of Troll and scorpion territory. They would have to return this way though. That gave Queen Nabila the chills. Perhaps the Dwarves or Elves knew of another way to return home.

Teyrnon flew to the outskirts of the next forest, it was up in the mountains higher than the last one. There was a welcomed drizzle. Queen Nabila, Anna and George stood looking into the forest, after getting off of the dragons, as the younger dragons entered the forest.

"Let's follow." George took each of the women's arms and they made their way over fallen trees, and sticky bushes. Then they came to a tiny stream, there was a bridge made for small Dwarves and small people. The queen and Anna went over it, George walked through the stream following the dragons. Finally, they approached a little house made of stone.

There was a dwarf outside bringing in firewood to cook dinner, he saw the dragons and men approaching, dropped the wood and said, "Oh me, oh my, who might you be?"

The queen said, "I am Queen Nabila of L'Azure, these are my companions. We are in search of my son, the prince. We have come to tell you of our news in L'Azure and implore your help."

"Oh, I am Nubout Leatherjaw, just call me Nubout, you must come inside and have dinner with us. I will introduce you to the other two dwarves. There are only 3 of us here, so I don't know how we can be of assistance, but do come inside. Oh dear." He looked worried, "No room for dragons in the house."

"Not a problem, they will find shelter out here." Queen Nabila walked up behind Nubout and helped him pick his wood back up.

"Oh my, no, no, you are a queen. I can get this." Nubout picked up the wood faster.

George grabbed some wood off the pile while the queen just let out a little sigh of relief, they would be safe tonight.

Once inside, Nubout introduced the Dwarfs to the queen and her companions. There was Gloriddeg Minebreaker, this was Andorlir Night-Brew's wife, Nubout was a nephew, there was a village of dwarfs down the road. This was a relief to the queen that these were not the only 3 dwarfs left.

After dinner, George and Andorlir went outside to see that the dragons were taken care of. Teyrnon had found a cave close by and they had made it comfortable for the night. The young dragons had brought in some plants to eat too. Andorlir gave them some left over fish from dinner. George explained that the next day, they would go to the village and talk to the dwarves there. Andorlir thought that they could all help in some way.

The drizzle was quite heavy the next morning as the dwarfs, the queen, Anna and George went into the town. Andorlir called a town meeting, everyone came, even the teenage dwarfs. Queen Nabila told them of their plight and how this evil king was going to destroy all of their land too. That got everyone talking.

"I say we go to L'Azure and help the dragons fight off this king. Then the Elves can come back with the future King!" That was the town mayor, Diggle Miner.

Everyone agreed. It was decided, because dwarfs decide things their minds don't change easily, they would leave day after tomorrow for L'Azure. They knew of the scorpions, but they knew the Scorpion King. He was half human, half scorpion, there was a spell on him, it had been placed on him when he was a child. He would want to help too, that might break his spell. Queen Nabila gulped, she didn't want scorpions in her kingdom.

"Excuse me, if the Scorpion King helps, with the scorpions we saw, umm come with him? Can they be trusted?" she asked.

"Yes, they can be trusted with friends. They will not befriend the evil king." Diggle Miner said, everyone agreed.

"Ok, it's decided then. We will get supplies tomorrow. You are welcome to stay until we leave." Andorlir said, "Let's go tell the dragons."

50

SOPHIE, JENNIE, LEILA, and Kanani went in search of Gunther, to see when he wanted to leave. They found him waiting for them by his cave. They had the dragons follow them to their homes, so they could grab some supplies for the trip. When that was done, Sophie and Kanani got back on Gunther. Leila and Jennie got onto Drake's back, and they took off. The dragons flew over the water towards the Land of L'Azure, Sophie smelled the air and hugged

Kanani, giving her a kiss.

"We will be happy staying in Camelot, Kanani. John is becoming a distant memory, I wasn't with him very long. That was another life, I love this one just as much." Then Sophie kissed her dog.

Kanani couldn't agree more with what Sophie said, this was a dog's life. Too bad Titus couldn't come with them, he had stayed with Lamorak's mom, it was lonely being an only German Shepherd. She thumped her tail.

"Hey you two on my back, what is going on?" Gunther asked. "Are you enjoying the view ahead of us?"

Sophie looked up, "Yes, Gunther, the land is beautiful, do you know where to fly?"

"I think so Sophie, let's get to that hill and stop, then we can regroup." Gunther flew ahead of Drake and led him to the cliff ahead.

As they got closer to the landing, Sophie held her breath, it was so beautiful! Then she saw something that took her breath away!

51

GUNTHER SAW IT TOO as he landed! They saw the famous red dragon, Y Ddraig Goch!!!

She is beautiful! Gunther whispered under his breath, but of course Sophie heard him.

Drake had trouble landing because he was staring at Y Ddraig Goch. They landed near her.

Sophie was worried about landing too close to this famous dragon, that no one had ever seen. This dragon had a reputation of importance, but she was a recluse living here all on her own. Sophie wasn't sure they should trust her yet. Sophie, Jennie, Leila, and Kanani got off the dragons.

"Sophie, is she safe to be around?" Jennie asked.

"I don't know." Sophie whispered back. "She doesn't look mean and she isn't looking angry. Look at our boys. He he." Sophie put her hands over her mouth to stifle a laugh. "That is the cutest thing."

Kanani wagged her tail and sat down next to Gunther.

As Gunther approached the red dragon he introduced himself, "My name is Gunther, this is Drake and this is Kanani, we are on our way to help find the lost Prince of L'Azure!"

"Lost Prince? Hmm, that is interesting. I have heard that there is a lot of turmoil in L'Azure. I heard the Queen fled from her nephew that took the crown. The Queen and King have always been good to the dragons. Oh, my name is Ddraig, it's nice to see someone. I'm pretty lonely living here in my cave, looking over the water. Who are the humans?"

"Sophie is the one that got off me, her sister Jennie and niece, Leila, were on Drake."

Sophie, Jennie and Leila walked over and stood by their dragons.

"Nice to meet you." Sophie said.

"Yes, it is indeed." Jennie chimed in.

Leila just waved.

"Would you like to come to my cave and have dinner. You can stay there and then be off in the morning. I have only one request." Ddraig waited.

"What is the request Ddraig?" Sophie asked.

"I would like to come with you. I have been here too many years on my own. The last of my kind died 20 years ago. I was afraid to leave, I didn't know where to go." Ddraig lowered her head.

Sophie looked at Jennie, Jennie nodded.

"You are welcome to come with us to find the Prince and to escort him back to L'Azure. Thank you for the offer of a place to stay. We will take you up on that as well." Sophie walked over and put her hand on Gunther. "That's ok with you isn't it, Gunther?"

"Yes! Yes, it is indeed." Gunther grinned as well as a dragon can.

Gunther had trouble keeping his elation out of his gait as he walked. They followed Ddraig to her cave, over the beautiful cliff above the L'Azure sea.

Sophie looked at the beautiful sea, the coastline and thought of her other life. Was this real? Could it be real? Had she ever been married to John? Then it hit her again, he hadn't been born yet and neither had she. Sophie had Lamorak's help with telling his mother how old she was, what year she had been born, that was tricky. Was this all wrong? Now she had her sister and niece living this lie too, not to forget Jennie's husband, Richard, all of them. Sometimes this just got the better of her.

"Sophie!" Jennie put her arm around her sister. "You are daydreaming again, sister."

"Oh." Sophie shook her head to clear her thoughts. "I was just admiring the beauty and thinking about our past lives, Jennie. Jennie, is this wrong? Should we go home?" Sophie had really gotten herself upset.

"You know we have talked about this before. We made a decision to stay. How could we live with dragons and knights if we went home? This is home, Sophie, this is home. I don't think you could adjust with modern times if you went back. Is it the marriage that is scaring you? Do we need a trip back to our time before you make this leap? Would Lamorak ever go back with you?" Jennie asked.

"I don't know, Jennie." Sophie wiped a tear from her eyes. "I have never asked him, maybe I should."

"Yes, maybe you should, sweetheart. Come on, we have an adventure to get on with. Who gets to sleep with the famous Red Dragon? WE DO!" Jennie laughed.

Sophie got her smile back and put her arm through her sister's. Gunther was walking next to Ddraig and Drake was trailing behind. Leila joined her mom and aunt.

"Mom?" Leila asked.

"Leila?" Jennie teased.

"Could I ride Ddraig? She asked if I would like to. She is very sweet, she has been so lonely. I can't wait to hear her story tonight." Jennie grinned at her mom and aunt.

"How can you say no, Jennie, look at Leila and look at that darling dragon." Sophie laughed.

"If you feel safe riding her, by all means. Poor Drake has had a lot of weight to carry with all of our bags too." Jennie kissed Leila on the cheek. "Go on, tell her yes."

"Oh Mom, thank you!" Jennie hugged her mom and took off to tell Ddraig the great news.

After unpacking, the camp fire was glowing, everyone settled down telling stories. Sophie played her violin for a bit as well. Ddraig told us her story.

"I was born on this island, the L'Azure Kingdom, my ancestors' were used by the men across the water to do battle for them to conquer land and find the Destiny Sword. My grandfather took my mother and father and brought them here, thinking that we would be safe from men. However, we weren't safe and then my mother was captured by men. They took her far, far away, my father followed to rescue her. They never came back, so after a while my grandfather took off to find them. He returned alone, broken hearted. He stayed for a few years, then told me he had to return to Scotland, I could go with him or stay. I chose to stay, I was too young to really make that kind of decision, I should have gone. I can only remember some of his stories, the last time he left me, he never returned. I couldn't go find him, I didn't know where to begin, so I stayed. No one ever came back for me and no one has ever visited, except all of you. I am very thankful, please don't leave me alone. Am I the only red dragon left in the world? Do you know?" Ddraig asked.

"We won't leave you alone and there are no red dragons left in the world, except you; and if you were caught, they would kill you out of fear and ignorance. The legend is that the great red dragon, Ddraig, fought the great white dragon for the passage way to the Sword of Destiny, that the greedy men wanted. The white dragon won and buried the red dragon in a cave." Gunther finished.

"There are no red dragons, except me then." Ddraig lowered her head and a tear rolled down her face.

"So, your name means red dragon, you need a real name." Gunther paused.

"Yes, I do need a real name, I love the name Ddraig, but it's every red dragon's name. Do any of you have a suggestion?" Ddraig asked.

"We will brainstorm and think of something, but back to the end of the red dragons. That must be when all of the dragons came to the town of L'Azure and befriended the king, guarding the land. They mustn't have known about you. They wouldn't have left you here alone. Say, how about the name, Keeva?" Sophie asked.

Ddraig's face lit up, "I like that, Keeva." she pronounced.

Gunther chimed in, "Keeva Ddraig, the beautiful red dragon."

Keeva liked that and so did everyone else. Tomorrow they would take off and hopefully meet up with Gunther's cousin, Teyrnon.

Sophia only wondered what was ahead of them on this journey, she wondered how they were going to find the other dragons and prince. Sophia was awake most of the night, she was already up when the others woke and had breakfast ready.

52

QUEEN NABILA, George, and Anna said good-bye to Andorlir and the others the next morning. They had a long day's trip ahead to find the prince, but Teyrnon had his cousin, Gunther arriving, hopefully with some men from Camelot. Queen Nabila wanted to know where they were going to meet them.

"That is a good question, I think we should wait here, in town. Andorlir and the men of the town left this morning, but Gloriddeg said we could stay. It might make the women dwarves feel safe having us wait here. Can you ask Gloriddeg, Queen Nabila or George?" Teyrnon asked.

"Yes, I can, but don't worry about where we sleep. I think we should find a spot we are visible, incase Gunther flies overhead, so we don't miss him." Queen Nabila answered thoughtfully.

"Oh, that does make more sense. Ok, let's go find our spot. I imagine Gunther will have to fly over this village to find us anyway." Teyrnon muttered while they walked from Gloriddeg's house and through the village to the other side. There was a stream and field, with plenty of visibility to spot anyone and they were very high up in altitude.

"What did you put in your message to your cousin?" asked Queen Nabila.

"I explained where I thought the young prince was, that they could meet us on the way or there." Teyrnon hesitated, "I said that we were leaving from L'Azure towards the dwarf village, so he will know to look for us and should find us here. If he doesn't come in a day or so, we should move on."

"Very good." The Queen said. "Let's get set up for the evening, it's beautiful around here. Come with me Anna, let's explore the pasture and woods behind them."

"Now you be careful." George said, "Perhaps I should go with you, better yet. Machel, would you mind going with them?"

"Not at all." Machel walked over to the queen. "My Lady, let us depart." Then he trotted beside the Queen.

While the queen was admiring all of the beautiful flowers, Machel kept watch all around them. Not being from this land, he didn't know what dangers might exist. It was a good thing he did, because as they got out in the middle of the field, arrows were being shot at them!

"My Lady, get on me!" Machel lowered his body. Both women got on his back and Machel took off. He scanned the scene from below as he flew over the field, the bowmen were in the tree line. Who were they? He had to make sure the queen was safe, so he flew back to their camp.

"George!" Gasped Queen Nabila, sliding off Machel. "Someone was shooting arrows at us! Machel saved our lives. Thank you Machel."

"Your welcome my Lady, but there is imminent danger. The bowmen are across that field." Machel looked to see if they were coming out of the trees.

"This is not good." Teyrnon looked angry.

"Albe keep watch here, Machel, come with me." Teyrnon looked at the Queen, "You will be safe with Albe, we will see what is going on. We may need to depart."

Anna hugged the Queen and George stood next to them. They were frightened.

Teyrnon and Machel took flight. As they got near the forest, they saw men with horses hiding behind the trees. When the men saw the dragons, they shot off arrows at them. Teyrnon turned to go back and just outside the forest, he swooped down and spit fire along the tree line. The men screamed, the horses whinnied and they pulled back further into the woods. Then the dragons flew back to their camp, reporting what they seen.

"It must be Arden's men! How dare he!" shouted the Queen. "We must warn the townspeople and depart from here as soon as possible!" Queen Nabila started picking up the camp.

"Yes," George ripped down the tent, got

everything packed, loaded the dragons and then they walked into the village to let the dwarves know of the danger. Gloriddeg was at the market.

"Thank you for letting us know, we will get the others that did not leave and protect our town, they will not get past us. You must go, now!" Gloriddeg told the Queen, she hurried out of the market and spread the news.

Photo by Lou Goetzmann on Unsplash

Teyrnon, Albe, Aedan, and Machel flew out of town with everyone on board. They flew towards the mountains. Finally, Teyrnon knew the Queen must be getting tired so he found a grove of trees with a spring to put down for the night. They made camp but Teyrnon kept looking for his cousin, Gunther, in the sky.

"I think we should stay here until Gunther from Camelot arrives," Teyrnon told the others.

The Queen didn't mind, they had plenty of food, they were out of danger.

The next morning went with nothing out of the ordinary, but the next morning when they woke up, they were covered in a blanket. The tops of the trees had been completely covered by a spider web!!!

53

"SOPHIA, YOU look worried." Jennie noticed that Sophie was being quit.

They were flying away from the coast and the red dragon's home.

"I am worried, I see no sign of Gunther's cousins. We should have told Merlin about this trip, I'm afraid he will find out and be cross." Sophie sighed.

Let's go down lower and take a look at the that! Gunther said.

Sophia looked down below them, there was a forest, but it was covered in white!

"Jennie, see I had a reason for concern, look down there!" Sophie pointed to the tree tops.

"Sophie! I see I should have listened to you before we left!" Jennie tensed up and Drake looked back at her concerned.

"Mom, Keeva is worried about landing by this forest, but she is getting tired. She is not used to flying long distances." Leila petted her dragon.

We must land and give Keeva a rest, Drake keep a look out for anything out of the ordinary, aside from the cobweb over the forest. Gunther was giving direction to the others.

I see a big spider over there! Drake roared.

"I see it too!" Sophia was getting a bit panic stricken.

"Mom, Keeva needs a rest, is this safe?" Leila pleaded.

"I don't know, but we must land. The dragons have fire they can fight the spiders off with! Right Drake?" Jennie was thinking solutions.

Drake didn't answer but roared and fire made some spiders disappear, but more came out of the trees. Gunther joined in and took a few more spiders out. They could hear cries for help under the web.

54

THE KNIGHTS from Camelot landed on the shores of L'Azure, they unloaded the horses and made camp. They planned on going to the dragons' side of the Town of L'Azure, that was at least a two-day journey without any interruptions. However, that night a rider came into camp. He told them of the great battle and how he and his men needed their help to save their King. They said that the King was still alive and had been taken hostage! He was being held by the direct orders of King Arden! Queen Nabila and the people were told her husband was killed, Agalone thought his father had been killed too. King Harlon was hidden on an island next to this one in a run-down dungeon and ruined castle. Arden knew all along that the King was not dead, he had this plot in his heart for years. He had secured this castle with no knowledge of the people of L'Azure. It was an old castle that was inhibited by a minor Lord, Arden had offered him enough money to buy it. There was talk of Arden hunting for the young prince that the Queen was searching for and having him killed too. The inhabitants of L'Azure which included the Elf's, Dwarves, the Black and White Dragons were all being summoned to defend the threat of Arden taking over their lands as well. They would secure Prince Eamon's safe return. However, they needed help in saving the king and his son, the prince, they were alive! When the tale was finished the knights fell silent.

Then the knights looked from one to

another, they told the rider that they would help, they decided to free the King and Prince first, then to ride on to L'Azure and stand with the others.

The next morning the knights took off at daylight, they would have to take boats to the tiny island where the king was being held hostage. There was no time to waste, lives were at stake.

55

TEYRNON ROARED and told everyone to stand back, then he let out a fire from his mighty dragon lungs and the web broke open. Anna was holding onto the Queen, George was protecting the women for any unforeseen spiders. Gunther and Drake were scorching the spiders, Sophia, Leila, Jennie and Keeva were keeping a distance from all of the fighting going on.

"I wouldn't live here at all!" Sophie cried looking horrified. "We don't have all of this in Camelot! Keeva, you must come home with us!"

I want to go home with you, I couldn't live here either. Keeva curled up next to Sophie. They thought the spiders would never give up, but at last Teyrnon, Machel, Albe, Gunther and Drake killed them all. George ran out from under the forest cover with the Queen and Anna.

Sophia ran over to the Queen and bowed before her. Queen Nabila would have none of that and told her to stand up.

"I am so very sorry for your losses, I hope that with our help we can bring your Prince safely back to L'Azure." Sophie said softly to the Queen, then she looked back at Jennie and motioned her to come forward as well.

"I appreciate all of the help I have gotten from Camelot and surrounding lands. We will take our town back and keep the dragons land safe." Queen Nabila shivered.

"Here my Lady," Anna brought a wrap to put around Queen Nabila's shoulders.

"Thank you, that helps, well, we must get

to Elf land by tonight to be safe. I will let Teyrnon and Gunther take it from here." The Queen said.

"Yes, we must get going, Keeva, are you rested?" Sophie asked the red dragon.

Yes, much better, I'm ready to move on. Keeva answered.

Sophie hugged Kanani, "What a good girl you are being."

Kanani knew she was being good, but only wagged her tail.

That night they flew up towards the mountain and then landed, the dragons walked for a while until they came to a nice cave with a waterfall. Everyone rested for the night. Gunther and Teyrnon had a lot of catching up to do. In the early morning light, they were awakened by none other than the Wizard Meuric!

After everyone was up, Meuric talked to the Queen and others, he said the young prince was aware of his heritage now, that he was a fine young man, he would make a strong, kind king.

He had been raised well, the only thing that was asked from his foster parents were that they were allowed to come and live with him in the castle part of the year. He was after all, like their very own son.

Queen Nabila had tears streaming down her face as she said, "Of course they can. I have dreamed of my son for all of these years. If I could go back and do it again, I would have changed my world. Arden would not have been brought into our castle, Eamon would have stayed with me, my beautiful Aclamet would be alive and my husband as well. This is reality though and the way it is, my Kingdom has been ravished by a traitor, my subjects are in danger of extinction. The choices I made then, I won't make again. To hold my son in my arms again…" Then she caught her breathe to hold back the sob in her throat and shook her head, she couldn't say anything more.

Meuric put his arms out and hugged her, "It will be fine, I will be with Eamon and you too, till the end of time."

That seemed to cheer her a bit, Sophie wiped the tears from her face and looked at her sister. Jennie hugged her, "I know Sophie, it was awful losing John, but he is never coming back. It's time to move on."

Sophie wiped her eyes, "I know you're right, I have you, Kanani, Titus, Leila, Richard your husband, and my husband to be, Lamorak. Everyone I love is here, I couldn't go back in time and live in 2023. You know I have changed history by being in his life, he wouldn't have been alive to this age if he hadn't picked me up on the side of the road when I fell through time while innocently caving."

Jennie chuckled, "That is true, but the history is rewritten in the books of time. If we were to go back and look on the internet, Lamorak, Knight of the Round Table, his bio would be that he married a beautiful young lady from another land. They lived happily ever after, no one will know it should have been that he died at a young age for revenge by another man from another kingdom." Jennie smiled, "It is inevitable that history is changed, just a wee bit, with us from the future."

"I know you're right, OH! I forgot, Grandpa is here too." Sophie put her hand to her mouth to stifle a laugh. "I don't know why, but at times I have felt a little bit down, lost, I just can't get a grip on it. I'm always so happy and positive, but something is off." Sophie shook herself to shake off the shadow hanging over her.

"Ah, I need to snap out of it, we have lot to do. We have to save a Prince and the Kingdom of L'Azure!"

"That's my sister!" Jennie gave her a high five.

"Mom! What are you and Auntie Sophie talking about?" Leila walked over to them.

"Saving a Prince and Kingdom, by love." Jennie kissed her cheek.

"Oh, Mom and Auntie, I love you guys." Leila blushed.

"Come on, we are leaving, pick up your things. How is traveling on Keeva? She is really a sweet dragon, isn't she?" Jennie asked.

"She is sweet, I can't believe she has been alone for years. I'm so glad we found her." Leila started packing her garments as she talked. "There, I didn't bring much, I'm ready."

"That's amazing, Leila!" Sophie laughed.

"I know, right? I usually overpack, but I'm growing up." Leila threw the bag over her shoulder and called Keeva over.

They took off from the cave and let Meuric the Wizard lead the way to the Queen's son. As they flew around the mountains, Sophie looked out towards the sea. This was such a beautiful island, but the big spiders, and scorpions, were all created because of the Wicked Witch, and the curses she put upon anyone that opposed her. She would have to be dealt with soon. Sophie was pondering how that was supposed to happen, then Meuric spoke up. He was on Gunther with Sophie.

"I have heard that the Witch Mira has her liar on the other side of the black dragons, she has taken some dragon eggs and raised two dragons to do her evil work. We might have to deal with her when we enter the area of L'Azure. She is the one that has enchanted and put curses on this land."

Sophie turned and looked at him, "This is frightening, the men from Camelot do not know this and they are coming over from England to this land. What if they walk into a massacre?" Sophie was visibly shaken.

"First of all, the dragons are in place, the white dragons and black, have been called to arms in our behalf. We might even meet up with them on our journey. The Dwarves have incorporated the Scorpion King to help fight. He is doing this to try and get the curse taken off of him.

He is hoping the Wicked Witch is there, he is ready to deal with her. The venom from his soldiers could kill her, if they could get close enough. I have called on your Merlin to come to us, he should be with the Elves by now. I feel confident that good will conquer evil. Arden apparently has been conspiring with Witch Mira for a long time, it's too bad that Eamon's older brother and father were killed." Meuric shook his head and paused a moment, then looked up and pointed, "Well, look, we are almost there!"

Queen Nabila looked very excited and nervous, her maid, Anna didn't look too excited. That made Sophie ponder, why?

"Put down over there!" Meuric pointed for the dragons to follow his command. Everyone landed in a soft meadow, little yellowflowers were blooming and a soft breeze blew, there was a strong odor of something delicious cooking.

Threwien, Eamon Aerendly, (Threwien's wife), and some of the neighbors were waiting for them. Meuric escorted the Queen over and introduced her to Threwien, Aerendly and Eamon. When she got to Eamon, tears started down her cheeks.

"Oh, my son, you look so much like your father." Meuric came over and put his arms around her. Then to everyone's surprise, Eamon took her hands.

"Mom, I have always suspected I wasn't an elf and adopted. I know you did what you had to do, but I have very loving parents here. I can't leave without them. I....." Eamon was interrupted by Nabila.

"I know, Meuric told me. I would be honored to have them come with us, my son." Then Nabila smiled.

Aerendly invited everyone to a big gathering and dinner. A roasted boar was on the pit outside, there were tables set up that were loaded with cooked fish, berries, apples, there was also some mung beans cooked up and nuts. There was an area set up for the dragons with tons of veggies and fruit. Neighbors poured red wine, berry juice and water. They had music playing in the background too. Leila and Eamon were seated next to each other, being about the same age. They hit it off talking of many things. Leila could tell a great story and not give herself up as a time traveler. This put Sophie and Jennie at ease, because that would just open up a can of worms, they weren't ready to deal with tonight.

As the feast continued, no one was aware of the fact that Anna had disappeared for quite a while. Sophie was looking for the Queen, then she looked around for George and couldn't find Anna, so she leaned over and whispered to Jennie. "Keep your eyes open for Anna, she is acting strange, Jennie."

"Yes, I will, I noticed something going on with her as well. Hey! Where is Kanani?" Jennie asked looking under the table and behind them, then over among the dragons.

"I thought she was with Gunther and the dragons!" Sophie got a worried look on her face and excused herself from the table. Jennie followed.

"Jennie, look!" Sophie pointed, Anna was walking back into the town and Kanani was hiding and following her. "Let's sit back down, hurry!"

"Sophie, Kanani is on her trail. That's wonderful. I wonder where Anna went? Here comes Kanani now.

"Kanani, good girl, where have you been girl?"

Sophie looked her dog in the face.

Kanani smiled and gave Sophie her paw. I wish I could tell you what I know Sophie. Next time I'll bring you along.

"I swear Sophie, it's like she talks to you." Jennie laughed.

"I know she does." Sophie rubbed Kanani's ears.

Anna was hanging back behind the dragons, that girl was up to something! Sophie thought.

There was a place for Sophie, Jennie and Leila to sleep in Threwien's brothers house. The Queen was put up in her son's house, George and Anna were with another relative. Before they all said goodnight, Sophie approached George and told him of the suspicions Kanani, Jennie and she had of Anna. He agreed that she was acting strange and that he had noticed some things in L'Azure too, now that he thought about it. Anna was friendly with Arden!

"So, either she is telling Arden where we are or she is doing something else wicked!" Sophie was displeased.

"Yes, I'm afraid so. I will keep watch tonight, all of us need to be on watch tonight, I'll let Threwien know. Thank you for coming to talk to me." George took off in search of Threwien.

In the middle of the night, Anna snuck out of the house. She looked around, George was still sleeping, she quietly closed the door and keeping in the shadows slipping out of town. Down the road there was a horse waiting for her, beside the horse was her love, Arrac, his mother was the wicked Queen Mira and she was a witch. Queen Mira favored King Arden, she had decided that it was getting too dangerous to leave Anna with Queen Nabila any longer. Queen Mira, and her son, Prince Arrac could use Anna now to proceed in the plan to take over the land of L'Azure.

56

THE NEXT MORNING George barged into the house Sophie was staying in, "Miss Sophia!" he cried.

"George! What has happened?" Sophie ran over and put her hand around his.

"Anna disappeared in the night! I didn't hear her, I have searched everywhere and she is nowhere to be seen. I don't know how to break this to the Queen. Her heart has been broken enough." George dropped his head.

"I'll come with you to tell her, give me a moment." Sophie went into the bedroom and got Jennie up, telling her what had happened as Sophie dressed.

Pretty soon Sophie came out with Jennie trailing behind her. "I'm ready George, Jennie needs to get Leila up and we need to see what the plan is for leaving." Sophie turned to Jennie, "I'll be back."

Jennie hugged her, "God speed sister." Jennie let Sophie go and watched her leave the house.

Sophie and George entered the house of Threwien, they explained to him what had just occurred and said they needed to speak to Queen Nabila.

The Queen came out dressed casually in a pale blue dress and shawl, "Good morning," she said.

"Good morning, my Queen, I'm afraid we have a situation, can we sit down?" George asked.

The queen looked at Threwien, "Of course sit down, let me get some food out." Threwien pulled out a chair for the queen and then took off toward the kitchen to find his wife.

After George told Queen Nabila what had happened, she was in disbelief!

"George, are you sure she was working with Arden? I wonder how many more of my servants are spies?" The Queen just shook her head in disappointment.

Threwien and his wife brought out food and tea, Prince Eamon came out with them to sit at the table. They were filled in as well to the situation, it was decided that they must pack today and start the long journey. There is another way back to L'Azure, not the way you traveled, but an Elf trail, we have it carved out in the mountain and outside as well.

We can travel through the mountains part of the way, then there is a passage around the rest of the lower mountains. We must pack food and warm clothing, we must take weapons, we are at war! Meuric must be consulted!" Threwien stood up, excused himself and went in search of the wizard.

Wizard Meuric was found outside by the dragons, he was greeting his friend Merlin, from Camelot. They were told of the treason and right away knew that they were going up against the Wicked Witch Queen, Mira! This was going to be a war of wars!

57

THE KNIGHTS of Camelot got out of the small wooden boat along the shore. Then they followed the riders from the night before, up the hill. The castle loomed in the distance, it was made of rock, had two towers and no wall around it. They snuck up the hill, there were guards, Lamorak shot his arrow and killed one, then the other guard called out an alarm. Two more guards came out of the castle, the Knights rushed them and engaged in a terrible sword fight, but in the end killed the opposing guards. The rider, whose name was Pamadis the Warrior, and his men rammed the castle door, the wooden door cracked and split apart, leaving an opening for the Knights to enter. Pamadis and his men led the way, they finally went down into the dungeon and found the King and his son. King Harlon had a chair in hand ready to fight, he put it down when he realized they were being rescued. King Harlon and Prince Agalone had not starved, but they weren't in the best of health after being kept captive here for so long.

"We must make haste and leave before more guards come to relieve the ones we killed!" Pamadis shouted.

The men helped the King and Prince out of the castle, without incident, they were in the boats soon after and had just landed on the distant shore, when they saw in the distance men riding. The men mounted their horses and prepared for battle. The men approaching saw the large group in the distance and turned around, fleeing back the way they had come.

They rode very fast and rode right into town to the castle, to let the King know of approaching soldiers. Arden was meeting with the newly arrived Queen Mira, they were making plans. Arden had the men go back and close the gates to the city, the only way they could be breached was by water.

Pamadis the Warrior and his men, the Knights of Camelot, The King of L'Azure and the Prince of L'Azure took the cut off and crossed over towards the dragon land. When they got closer to the dragons, they were amazed to see the armies there already! The Scorpion King and his scorpion men, the Dwarves, the White Dragons and Black Dragons, old and young. Emmorous met them and was ecstatic to see the King still alive and Prince Agalone as well. They were told that the Elves had started the journey here with the Queen and young Prince Eamon. They would be shocked and pleased to see that Harlon and Agalone were still alive! They had enough of them here now to start the fighting, they would start first thing in the morning. The wicked Queen Mira was there with her son, she had turned the Scorpion King and his scorpion men in to half men many years ago. The curse needed to be broken, the kingdom and people needed to be set free of all this evil.

That night there was music, food, plans were made, and talk, a lot of talk about what the morning would bring. The next morning, they were awakened early with King Arden had his men shooting fireballs out of slings towards the other shore. None had reached shore yet, but the men got ready, with their slings and bows to fight back, the dragons lined up and spit fire across the water. It made Arden's men back up a bit, but they were getting a boat in the water now! Queen Mire stood in it and used her magic, she made a big cloud around herself, Arden, and his men.

As they put boats in the water, Emmorous looked around, "Where is Meuric the Wizard?" he shouted.

Someone shouted out, "Coming with the

Elves, should we send help to get them here sooner?"

"Yes!" Was the answer Emmorous replied with.

The dragons looked at each other, it was decided that 3 of them would take off and go around the

other side of the mountain, the Elf Trail and look for them.

In the meantime, the warrior Pamadis, his men and the Camelot Knights were the only men able to fight. The dragons could spit fire, but fight the magic of Mira was impossible. The scorpion men could only do harm if they were close enough, so they got into the river and put up a wall against the shoreline. Mira didn't move her boat any closer, but held her ground. Four dragons took flight and flew over the city of L'Azure, they took in the site below. There were many peasants that were trying to leave the town out of the back gates. Arden had another King and army with him, helping him fight. The dragons let out a roar and fire spit out on the town, the people scattered that weren't running, the armies of men put up their shields, but they were melted. Several died, some took cover. The dragons flew back and gave a full report of what they saw and the results of their attack. Lamorak, his fellow knights, and Pamadis the Warrior, got on some freshly rested dragons. They flew over the Queen in her boat, then shot arrows down upon the troops, the men on the ground shot arrows up towards the dragons. Lamorak's dragon took a hit and fell from the sky. His dragon was hurt, but they needed to get out of there. Seeing one of their own down, the dragons swooped down and one on each side grabbed the fallen dragon, flying him back to the other shore. Another dragon landed to get Lamorak, but there was an on slot of arrows firing at him, so Lamorak had to turn and fight. Pamadis the Warrior jumped off his dragon and stood beside Lamorak, they fought a bloody battle, Lamorak was one of the greatest Knights of the Round Table! He was skilled with his sword, but the knight he was fighting had a grudge against him. His name was Enid and he was determined to kill Lamorak for revenge of Lamorak's father killing their father, King Agravaine Orkeny. It was just luck that Lamorak was here for this terrible injustice to be done. On the other side of the water when the wounded dragon was taken back more dragons, men, dwarves and company flew over the water to do fight. They saw the mighty battle between Erec, Enide, Lamorak and Pamadis. The dragons landed and the soldiers jumped off, joining the fight. It was a terrible battle; one dwarf was wounded and drug back to a dragon to get aid. Lamorak and Pamadis were tired, they were starting to miss, the new knights came in and took over, but Enide took off after Lamorak, without Lamorak knowing and stuck a sword into his back. The armor cracked, the sword went through and hit him above the heart, he stood there a minute, then dropped to the ground. Pamadis and the knights slew Enide and Erec, then went over to the wounded Lamorak.

Gaheres knelt beside his friend, "Hold on,

we need to get you back to the other side."

Lamorak grabbed his friend, "Tell Sophia, that I love her, I am sorry." Then Lamorak closed his eyes and died in Gaheres arms.

Gaheres was in shock, Pamadis came over and knelt by his friends, looking at Gaheres, he said, "This can't be true, it just can't be."

"Pamadis, these brothers have been after Lamorak for years, Lamorak's father killed their father in a battle, it was an accident. Lamorak's father was murdered and they swore to kill his son. Lamorak should not have come over here. King Arthur will be very upset. Come, help me load him on my dragon, let's get him back to our side." Gaheres looked around, the battle was still raging, but he had to get Lamorak out of here.

As the dragons landed and the still body of Lamorak was seen by the men of Camelot, there was disbelief and sadness. Richard lifted his friend off of the dragon and placed him inside Teyrnon's cave, the men gathered around him.

"Oh, Sophie, she is going to be devastated." Tears ran down Richards face as he went to clean up his friend and cover him up.

58

SOPHIE CLIMBED upon Gunther, everyone was ready and the march through the mountains was underway. There was a fairly large party, 10 elves, 2 wizards, 7 dragons, the prince, queen, George, Sophie, Kanani, Jennie and Leila. They would have been quite a site looking down upon them from the air. The mountain was cool inside, there was just enough room for the dragons to pass through and there was running water with fish to eat.

Sophie looked at Jennie, "I have this feeling something is off, remember I have had it for a while now, there is something off, Jennie."

"I feel it too Sophie, I think you've rubbed off me on. I hope the men are safe." Jennie added, then she was sorry she did because of the look on Sophie's face of worry. "I am sure they are fine, Sophie, come on, enjoy our trip. This is something we don't usually get to do." Jennie joked, trying to cheer her sister up.

"I feel it in my bones, my life is changing somehow. Let's go." Sophie got up and started walking, the dragons following them. Kanani was running up and down between everyone, having a grand time.

"There's the opening up there, we will have to journey on the outside of the mountain from here," Threwien announced.

On their 6th day of travel, as they left the

mountains and walked into the sun, they were met by several dragons that flew down to meet them.

It was announced that the fight had begun, the wicked witch Queen Mira was there fighting for the other side. They needed Meuric and Merlin now to help them. Traveling on the outside around the mountains would take 6 more days, so it was decided that the wizards would fly on ahead.

Sophie was really concerned now, "Can Gunther and I go with you?" Sophie pleaded.

"Sophie no," Jennie said, "We need to stay with the queen and elves, don't you think? The men don't want us in the fighting."

Meuric thought about it, "I feel that Prince Eamon needs to stay back with the elves and queen. If Sophie, Jennie and Leila want to come with us they can. It would lighten the load of the others traveling."

Sophie looked at Jennie, "Ok, Sophie,"

then she turned to look at Leila.

"Mom, I'm staying back with Eamon and the queen." Leila smiled and it melted Jennie's heart. Her girl was growing up.

"Ok, honey, I'm going on ahead with Sophie. Be careful." She kissed her daughter and turned to leave with her sister.

It took them a few hours of flying over the mountains to get over the pass, then get into the camp, as they flew down, Sophie looked around. The men of Camelot where here! There were a lot of critters and men here for this, it was rather exciting. Meuric and Merlin immediately took off towards the water to help fight with magic. Merlin flew on a dragon over Mira and broke her magic spell. It startled her and she threw a lightning bolt his way, she missed, Meuric was on another dragon and shot off a poison bolt at her. She screamed and fell out of the boat, Arden helped her get back in and they rowed to shore. Merlin and Meuric followed them and shot a few more, the dragons spit out fire. Some of the soldiers were burned to a crisp, the witch threw a shield around Arden and herself. The scorpions came across the water and up onto the banks. The Scorpion King stabbed a stinger into the queen. He immediately turned into a man. He was astonished! His scorpion men soldiers were all turned into men as well. There was a lot of confusion. The queen had been stabbed with poison, she was dying. Her son ran out to meet her and rubbed an herb on her wound. Then they carried her into the castle. The men were weaponless and had no clothes now, so they hurried back to the other side. The knights quickly gave them clothes. Merlin and Meuric hurried back to the other side as well.

Sophie, Kanani and Gunther went in search of Lamorak. Jennie found Richard and was talking to him, then Richard came over and took Sophie's arm.

"My dear, you must be strong." Richard took Sophie and put an arm around her shoulders.

"What is it Richard?" Sophie asked hesitantly.

"Lamorak has been killed." Richard held Sophie up.

Sophie's face was in shock, she started collapsing, then the sorrow and tears came, "No, no, Jennie, I told you I felt something." Sophie sobbed. "I want to see him, I want to see him," Sophie sobbed, trying to wipe away the tears so she could walk.

"Oh Sophie!" Jennie sobbed running to her.

"This way." Richard guided her into the cave.

There, on a blanket was her knight. Why had she waited so long to say yes to him? Then she remembered why, in history he was killed young. She looked up, "How? How did this happen?" Sophie cried, sobbing over Lamorak's still body. Kanani came over and put her paw on Sophie, then kissed her. Sophie put her arms around her dog. "Thank you Kanani, thank you."

Jennie was crying as she knelt down beside her sister and held her.

Richard explained how Lamorak was killed and who did it. Sophie just cried as Jennie said, "Honey, it's written in history that he was killed by those men, you couldn't change it."

King Harlon and Prince Agalone walked into the cave and approached Richard. They talked for a while, then Richard introduced Jennie and Sophie to both of them. Through her tears Sophie stood up to greet them.

Prince Agalone was good looking, he was tall, Sophie's age of 29, he had sandy hair and looked like a hunk, that is what Jennie was thinking.

King Harlon put his on Sophia's shoulders and told her how sorry he was, Prince Agalone came over and softly took Sophie's hand, he knelt and kissed it, then said, "I'm so sorry my Lady, thank you for coming to our aid, I am forever indebted to you. I'm extremely sorry for your loss."

Sophie looked down at him through her tears and said, "Thank you."

"Come, let's leave and gather, there is a meeting at the bonfire tonight, you need not stay here." Then Prince Agalone stood and took Sophie's hand to walk her out of the cave.

Sophie drank some wine, and clung to her sister; Prince Agalone never left her side. When it was late, he escorted her back to a sleeping place that was prearranged. Her sister, Jennie laid down beside her, Richard slept nearby. Kanani was sleeping next to Sophie. This was a surreal moment that would take a lot of effort to get over. Sophie only fell asleep as the sun was rising, she was in disbelief and she hurt so much. She was awakened by Kanani licking her. She just did not know how she could get up and start the day. The battle was still raging across the water. She could hear it. The men that had the scorpion curse on them, were all men now, the wicked queen was injured. How many would they lose today? That is all Sophie could think of. Jennie was already up and walked into the cave placing a cup of tea next to her.

"Can you get up sweetheart? I will help you dress and get cleaned up. We have lost some more men already this morning. I am worried sick about Richard, he has been mainly staying over on this side of the water helping direct the different strategies for winning." Jennie took Sophie's hand and helped her up.

"Thank you, sister. I must pull myself together for the others. Where is Prince Agalone? He was so kind yesterday." Sophie thought, "His mother, the Queen, should be here today, so should Leila, and Prince Eamon!" Sophie thought that was something to look forward to.

"Yes, they should be here today. I cannot wait to put my arms around Leila, I want all of you nearby, there is so much grief and danger all around." Jennie wrung her hands, she was so very worried about Sophie, Richard, and Leila.

Sophie came out of the cave and she saw Prince Agalone walking her way.

"Good morning my Lady, how are you feeling this morning? I have made sure that there was a good breakfast for you and Jennie, come with me. My mother shall be here shortly, I cannot wait to see her, oh and a brother I have not met, not since he was a baby." Prince Aclamet put his arm out for Sophie and the other for Jennie, then led them towards his camp.

The war waged on for another month. There were many more losses, Sophie was busy taking care of others to put her mind at ease, night time was the hardest of all. Prince Agalone kept a close watch on her while doing his duties. One morning Prince Agalone met Sophie as she had just gotten up. He told her there was good news and he led her to look over at the town.

"Many things have happened, I think the war will end soon." He looked at Sophie, "It has been wonderful to have you here, to help out, I mean." He blushed and looked away.

Sophie smiled, "It has been a pleasure for me to have you here also, to help with the hard times we are all going through."

He took her hand and gently kissed it, "Look," he whispered.

Sophie looked.

Across the water, The Dwarfs were leading an attack on the town, the townspeople had fled, except for the boys and men, they stayed behind and fought. The town people had run up into the hills behind L'Azure.

"I must find my father; would you like to come with me? Prince Agalone asked.

"Yes, I do!" Sophie smiled, grabbing his hand and running with him to his father.

Prince Agalone and the King talked, then started making provisions to rescue the townspeople and bring them over to the dragon's side of the water. Sophie excused herself to find her sister and have a quick breakfast, making some food for Prince Agalone too. He arrived to talk to Sophie about plans, while he ate.

They were just finishing with breakfast when a runner arrived into the Kings camp with news. Prince Agalone was keeping watch and excused himself. He went over to his father, he was not gone long and then came back to Sophie and Jennie.

"Well, Mira the wicked witch deserted! She wanted to go home, she lost her powers from the scorpion venom and insisted her son, Prince Aclamet, get her out of L'Azure. Arden fled with them, so the army that came to help him is now deserting too, their king was killed, and they are surrendering, they want to make peace and join us. Arden will have to be dealt with, but for now he is gone. When my mother arrives, we will go back to our castle, across the water, and see what needs to be done for the people." As he finished speaking, they looked around, there was cheering from across the water. The villagers were waving across the water at the King and dragons.

"Ha, look at that Sophie, its over!!!" Jennie hugged her sister.

Sophie wiped a tear from her face, "Yes, I'm so very happy it is. We will be able to go home now."

"Jennie looked at her, yes we will, it won't be the same, we will have to help you adjust."

Sophie shook her head yes, and looked out upon the water. Just then there was another commotion, Leila, the Elves and dragons were coming towards her, they had just arrived!!! She turned her head and waved at Leila. "Let's go get them!" Sophie said.

The queen got off the dragon and looked around, she could not believe her eyes! Running towards her was her HUSBAND AND SON! She fainted.

59

WHEN SHE opened her eyes, her husband was holding her. She was overjoyed with elation!

"What has happened?" Queen Nabila asked.

While King Harlon explained to his wife what had happened, her younger son arrived. Prince Eamon was introduced to his father and brother, then he introduced Threwien and Aerendly, the Elves that had raised him as their own. Prince Eamon looked around for Leila, he saw her talking to her mom and aunt, he excused himself to bring her over to introduce her to his father and brother. When he approached her, he saw that she had been crying.

"Leila, is everything ok? What has happened?" Eamon asked.

"Oh Eamon, Sophie's fiancé, Lamorak, was killed." Leila sobbed.

Sophie had started crying again too, Jennie was comforting her and Eamon was comforting Leila.

"This is tragic for sure, I'm so sorry, Sophie." Eamon grabbed her hand. "If there is anything, we can do to repay you, just ask."

Sophie shook her head and through a tearful voice, "Thank you Eamon, it will get easier, I just need to stay busy, Leila go meet Eamon's family."

Leila let go of Eamon and hugged Sophie and her mom, "I'll be right back." She promised.

Queen Nabia came over to Sophie with Leila and Eamon, "Sophie, I'm so sorry. You must be our guest when we get the castle back, it would be good for you to do something different. Agalone is going to be busy cleaning up the town and helping residents get their lives back, perhaps you can come back and help with that, if you would like to."

"That would be very therapeutic for me, after we go home, perhaps I can come back. "Sophie smiled.

"We are making a crossing into the town in a little while, would you like to come with us, Sophie?" Agalone asked.

"Yes, I would like that, let me clean my face and change my shoes." she said.

"I'll be over to get you in half an hour then." Agalone took his mother's arm and walked her back to camp.

"Sophie, he is so charming, Prince Charming," Jennie giggled.

"Stop that Jennie, I just lost my Lamorak, my heart is broken."

"I know that it is, but hearts have to mend, enjoy today, because they are getting the dead ready for the journey back to Camelot. We will be leaving in a couple of days' time." Jennie informed Sophie.

Sophie pondered all that Jennie had just said and thought about Nabila's offer to stay at the castle. A little burning desire had started in Sophie's heart.

A little while later...

Sophie and Kanani were on the boat with Nabila, Eamon, Agalone, George, Leila, Threwien, and Aerendly, (Eamon's surrogate parents.)" Gunther had insisted on going, so he was flying over to meet them when they got there. The town was in chaos, they had to fight their way through the throngs of people trying to touch the king and queen. They were so happy that the beloved kingdom would be restored! The party reached the castle. The king turned around and gave the people a speech.

I want to say that I never gave up trying to get home to all of you and my beloved Queen. (Here he held her hand and raised it high.) We are back! Both of my sons as well! We will restore the town, clean up the shambles. The Dragons and everyone from this Kingdom have come to our aid. We have proven that we are a Kingdom to be reckoned with. There will be news to come soon. Right now, we need to go inside the castle and see what we have in food and supplies to help all of out. Go to your homes if they are still standing, if not, come into the court yard, we will make temporary quarters for you until we can rebuild!

There was another cheer from the townspeople!

Sophie looked around, there was a lot of work to do. She was thinking that she would come back, but right now she had to go home and bury the dead. Tears fell from her eyes as she looked around, this was real, it was her life. She wiped them away as Prince Agalone walked over to her. He led her into the castle, it wasn't as bad as she had feared.

£

In the meantime, John was getting ready to return to Luxembourg soon, he had soaked up the sun on the Hawaiian beach and thought long and hard. Mike and John had long talks at night over dinner and a night cap. The plans were made, Mike was going to go with John to Luxembourg, then they would see about this venture to Camelot.

60

THAT NIGHT as Sophie and the others rode across the water on a boat back to the camp, she knew in her heart she would return and help. Prince Agalone rode back holding Sophie's hand. Sophie thought it felt good to hold his hand.

"Sophie, he said, "I have talked to my parents, I am going to accompany you home with your dead. Eamon and I will represent our Kingdom at the funerals, in thanks for what your men have done and died for. This will show respect to King Author, as well. I will speak to the Knights of the Round Table and see when they want to leave. My father will be back over in the morning to meet with the knights." Prince Agalone waited for this to sink into Sophie and see what she thought of it.

"I think it's an honorable thing to do, I thank you." Sophie squeezed his hand and kept hold of it, as they went across the water.

Not another word was said. They just took in the feeling of the evening, the peaceful water, the others were quite too. It was a bit surreal to comprehend. When they reached shore, men took the ties of the boat, Prince Agalone got off and helped Sophie out. Leila and Prince Eamon got off after them, Agalone and Eamon were going to stay in their camp for the night. They chatted as they walked up hill to the camp fires. Everyone was celebrating! They were offered food and drink; the dwarves had musical instruments and were playing tunes. Jennie walked over and handed Sophie a violin. To her delight Sophie took it. Prince Agalone looked at her in surprise as Sophie took the violin and started playing some Celtic fiddle tunes to match the dwarf's music. Sophie got carried away by her music, closing her eyes, events of time went by in her mind. She thought of John, Hawaii, the mysteries she had shared with Kanani and her friends. The years her sister was missing from her life, raising Leila, and then John missing and her mishap falling through time. Her decision to stay in this world. These dragons and men were her family now, how could she go home? She didn't know what her future would bring or how she would ever tell this prince beside her where she was really from.

61

THE NIGHT wore on and Sophie put the violin down. Prince Agalone looked at Sophia.

"How did I get so lucky to meet such a unique lady?" he asked.

"I hope you feel that way when you get to know me." Sophie laughed.

He looked at Sophie with amusement, Jennie interrupted by picking up Sophie's violin and giving her sister a look, which was a warning to not give too much information up.

"I think it's time we all go to sleep. My dear husband is already in bed, Leila, Sophie, let's go. Good night everyone, thank you for everything." Then Jennie turned and started walking off.

Sophie stood and looked at Leila, "Let's go, good night Agalone. He stood up and took her hand walking away from the others and then he KISSED HER!

To Sophie's surprise, she liked it, so she kissed him back, a long kiss. When she pulled back, he took her hands.

"Till morning my Lady." He bowed and watched her walk away.

Leila was staring at her aunt, "Aunt Sophie! Isn't he handsome and charming?"

"Yes, he is, Leila, yes he is." Sophie blushed and put her arm through her nieces' arm. She glanced back to see Agalone watching her. She waved and then turned around to go into her cave. Kanani was trotting beside her very happy and tired.

The days wore on with preparations on getting the dead home. A rider had left a week ago to let King Author know that some of his knights had been killed. That they would be bringing them home for a formal burial.

A few weeks later Sophie, Kanani and the others left for in Camelot. Sophie was having a lot of mixed feelings, it was surreal that Lamorak was gone. If only she had married him, a tear dropped down her cheek. That would have been changing who he was and his life line though, she would have rewritten the history of his life. What were the history books saying now about him? She would have to look that up. She needed to go home, she felt it in her heart, at least for a bit. Leila rode on Keeva with Prince Eamon, Prince Agalone rode on Cham. This gave the

Knights of the Round Table ample time to arrive ahead of them with the dead knights. When they arrived, Sophie went over to Lamorak's mother's house and picked up Titus. She was so happy to see him, but when she saw Lamorak's mother she lost it. His mother was very sad, but pretty much used to it, she had lost her husband in the same manner. Sophie stayed for a bit as they chatted, his mom wanted to know how it happened and Sophia made sure she knew that he died a hero.

A week later the funeral took place, it was a very hard day for Sophie. She had not slept the night before and had not stopped crying either. Jennie, was with her all night to give her support. Of course, Kanani and Titus did as well. Sophie didn't know if she could go through the funeral in the morning. Prince Agalone was staying in the castle, Sophie had not seen much of the prince. She felt good when he was near her, which made her feel so guilty, but her life had just been turned upside down! She was in another century, her first husband was killed serving America in a war, now her fiancée died fighting in his world saving a kingdom far away from his home. Now, really, she could go home, but then she thought of her dragon, she loved him and could not take him home. She wondered how long dragons lived, then let that thought go, she was really having a difficult time. The next morning, Sophie dressed in a long black dress and had a veil that was attached to a black hat with a large rim. Leila and Jennie had helped Sophie make the dress, hat and veil. Sophie didn't think it was how people dressed in this time period, but she didn't care. Perhaps she would start a trend in Camelot.

There were hundreds of people at the funeral, neighboring kingdoms and royalty were in attendance. Sophie and Kanani were allowed to walk behind Lamorak's casket. His fellow knights were the pall barriers, they were dressed in shiny black boots, they had a gold dragon emblem on their red vests, the top coats were long, falling below their knees, just above their boots. They looked very formal. Perceval,

Lamorak's brother was one of the pall bears, he had shed his tears, but his face was unreadable today.

King Arthur rode in front on his white horse, there were 6 knights on each side of the three knights that lost their lives. Lamorak's family was there, his mother was inconsolable. It made Sophie feel even more sorrowful. People threw flowers over the caskets as they passed, Sophie looked, her dragon had forced himself behind her. When she turned and saw him, it made her feel more comfortable. King Arthur honored the knights by putting their swords over them as they were buried. They were laid to rest inside the castle walls. Jennie put her arm around her sister, Sophia turned to her with tears in her eyes. "We haven't changed the future too much, have we?"

"No, Sophie, I don't think we have. He died young in the tales about Camelot, if you had married him, then I'm not sure how history would have been changed. Lamorak was a Round Table knight. Now, Prince Agalone from

L'Azure is not even in the history books! I don't think that would matter as much as marrying a King Arthur knight would, "Jennie smiled and gave Sophie a hug.

Leila came over and stood next to Sophie, taking her left hand, "I'm here for you Auntie."

"I know you are Leila, I can't thank you enough for that. Are you going back with Prince Eamon to help get his city and their people back together?"

"I would like to, what do you think?" Leila asked Sophie.

"I think you should and I think I will as well. I can't stay here right now, my heart hurts too much. Leila? First, I think we should do something before though. What about a quick trip home?"

"Auntie! Really? You haven't gone back for a long time." Leila squeezed Sophie's hand.

Sophie turned to her sister, "How about a quick trip back home?"

"Sophie! I haven't been back in years. I don't know, I will have to think about this and ask Richard. Have you heard from Kimo or Susan? They left a year ago to go back to Hawaii to visit his parents and they haven't returned?" Jennie asked.

"No, I haven't heard from them. You know, I'm getting a bit concerned, I think a trip back to Hawaii is in order. I know Kimo's parents." Sophie looked thoughtful. Turning back to Leila, she said, "I want to go to Hawaii, how about a vacation?"

"That sounds like a lot of fun, Auntie. What do we tell the L'Azure princes?" Leila asked.

"We tell them, we have some things to attend to and we will see them when we have things done." Sophie smiled through her tears.

The next day Sophie was walking with Prince Agalone outside of the walls of Camelot. She was explaining to him that she had some things to attend to and then she and Leila would be more than happy to visit them and help with the restoring of their kingdom. Maybe finding the evil queen, Mira and put her in prison. Prince Agalone had to laugh at that.

"You are the most wonderful woman I have ever met, my Lady. I will be waiting for the day you show up in my kingdom. Is there anything I can do to help you so you can come to me sooner?" he asked taking her hand and pulling her closer.

"No, I appreciate you asking this, but I must do this myself." Sophie smiled slyly.

"Ok, hmm, could you bring Cham back with you when you come visit? I know that Emmorous didn't want his young dragon to move away from home." He chuckled.

Sophie laughed, "That's funny. We will be sure to take him home when we visit."

Leila showed up with her mom, Jennie, and Prince Eamon, "Our ship is getting loaded for take-off right now." Prince Eamon told his brother. "I thought I would come and say good bye for now to you Sophia." Prince Eamon bowed to Sophie.

"Oh, thank you, Leila and I will be over to see you before you know it." Sophie said.

"Well brother, I guess this is it. I can't thank you enough Jennie and Sophie for your sacrifice coming to our aid. We have our kingdom back, we are a family once again. This is going to be a sorrowful good bye." Prince Agalone looked at Sophie hoping she would change her mind. Sophie let him give her hand a kiss. He wanted to really kiss her, but respected her dignity. She had just lost her fiancée after all. He would have to give her time to get over the hurt. Sophie wanted him to kiss her, but was glad that he didn't, she probably would have given in and gone with him.

Sophie, Leila, and Jennie watched their princes board the ship, Jennie took Sophie's hand, together they waved good bye. Agalone was standing on the back of the deck of the ship looking at Sophia until he was out of sight.

"Oh, I'm so sad and confused, let's go home and have a family dinner and talk about a trip to Hawaii." Sophie scratched Kanani's head as they walked for a bit, then she wiped a tear from her eyes.

£

Sophie had talked Leila into going back in time with her, but not her sister. Jennie would keep Titus and Sophie would take care of Leila. Jennie and Titus walked with Sophie, Leila, and Kanani to their rock across from the pub. Sophie kissed her puppy goodbye, hugged her sister and went behind the rock, she touched the rock, praying it still worked, and an opening appeared, she placed her foot out, felt the stone step, Leila, and Kanani followed her. They stood there, the rocked closed and they felt a surge of power shoot them forward, they fell out inside of an empty cave.

"Wow, things haven't changed Leila, have they? Sophie asked as she brushed herself off.

"Not really," Leila answered as she pulled her top down. They were dressed in clothes from their own time period.

They walked out of the cave with Kanani and got onto a bus that took them to the street of Sophie's bank. She pulled out some euros and then hailed a cab, which took them to their house. The cab driver eyed them warily, they were dressed in clothes from another time. Sophie told him they were actresses in a play. When they entered the house, Sophie didn't go into the kitchen, but into her room and changed into clothes she still had in her closet, luckily, they still fit, Sophie thought. She packed a few things in a bag and as Leila did the same. Then they got into the waiting cab for a ride to the airport. The flight to Hawaii was a long one, so Sophie took a nap. She had a lot to think through.

62

JOHN AND MIKE boarded Lufthansa to France in dock 22, Sophia walked off Lufthansa on the same day and same time, but in dock 56. Neither of them saw the other. Sophie felt a chill go through her. Leila glanced at Sophie wondering what she was thinking about. If only she was brave enough to ask. Sophie had lost John, then she lost the love of her life for the second time recently when Lamorak was killed.

£

John felt a chill as he boarded the airliner to take him home to France. He tried to make small talk out of it, but was having a difficult time. How could he even take up a normal existence again? He had PTSD now and noises bothered him, maybe going through time to see if Sophie was there and being in a different time would heal him. Mike looked at his friend with concern, John started talking about his time in captivity. He would have Sophie write a book about what he and his crew had gone through. Then he wondered if Sophie could write in another century without electricity and a computer. That kept his mind busy wondering different outcomes until he dozed off to sleep, dreaming of Sophie and Kanani.

John and Mike landed in Luxembourg that night. John rented a car and drove to his house. They stayed a few days, John didn't go into his room he shared with Sophie, so he didn't see her clothes. John and Mike took the car and John showed Mike around the town, and then over a cafe dinner they planned the trip back through time. The next morning they drove to the caves, arriving at the booth John had many questions for the ticket person.

"How can you charge to time travel? Do people from that time get to come here?" he asked.

"No, this is just for people from this time to go. There are very strict rules before you go. We have clothes that are part of the package, so you fit in, you must not let anyone know where you are from. It is a 42 hour pass you are looking at. It costs $500 Euros per person, this includes the clothes. You have a stamp and must come back on the date of the stamp or you will be tracked down and charged more or be stuck there forever with no return until you pay." The ticket person advised them.

John looked at Mike, "Well, should go for the fun of it?"

"Why not? You know that you might see Sophia, what will you do?" he asked.

"I don't know." John answered.

They bought the tickets, changed into time period clothes, opened the door and got into the elevator. John felt a panic attack coming on as the doors closed, but he took a deep breath and closed his eyes.

63

SOPHIE HOOKED Kanani's leash onto her and Leila grabbed their on board luggage. They walked out of the Maui airport and Sophie hailed a cab. They got in and she handed the address to the driver. He pulled up in front of a nice home, the ocean was in the back of the property, there was a beautiful rock garden in front with a flower bed of Plumeria, Hawaiian Hibiscus, Bird of Paradise, Pikake (Jasmine), Ohia Lehua, and Naupaka flowers. Sophie had forgotten that Kimo's parents made and sold Leis for a living. They were retired now, but maybe that is why Kimo and Susan didn't come back to Camelot? Maybe they had taken over the business.

Sophie approached the front door, it was a beautiful wooden home, the big double front doors were made of cedar. Sophie took the large pineapple knocker and tapped on the door. She looked around, it didn't look like anyone was around, maybe they were on the beach?

The door opened to her surprise, it was Kimo's mom. "Hi, Mama Kalani, it's Sophie!" Sophie put her arms out to hug Kalani.

"Oh my! Sophie and Kanani too, is that Leila all grown up? Come in, come in. Kimo and Susan will be so happy to see you!" she said hugging each of them in turn.

They entered the house. Sophie looked around, everything was so clean. She took off her shoes, as did Leila, then followed Kalani into the kitchen.

"You like some tea, dears?" she asked.

"Yes please, is Kimo or Susan here?" Sophie asked sitting down.

Kalani turned around, "They took a day trip to the other side, they should be home for dinner. They will be so happy to see you. Kimo was just saying that it was about time they returned to Luxembourg to see you, Sophie. This is such a nice surprise."

"Well, they are a bit overdue, we wanted to come to Hawaii anyway. May we take Kanani out to the beach?" Sophie asked.

"That would be lovely, let me get Kanani a drink first. We are doing a barbecue tonight, I have some things to make, why don't the three of you go down to the water. Here's some beach glasses for your drinks." She took out some unbreakable mugs out and poured the tea into it.

"Thank you," Sophie and Leila both said.

Sophie thought it felt good to be in the Hawaiian sunshine, in her own time. She was missing her puppy and Gunther, her dragon, but this was a good break. She had Kanani with her, that's all she needed tonight.

64

JOHN AND MIKE looked around them as they stepped out of the metal box. Up the road was a small village. So, they walked towards it and found a pub. (The pub that was across from Sophie's rock.)

They entered the pub and sat down, looking at the menu, John chuckled, "Let's have a real pub lunch my friend."

"Sounds fine to me." Mike licked his lips, "I'm hungry and thirsty."

The waiter approached and Mike ordered a cask of ale and the lunch special of crusty bread, cheese, light meats, peaches, and herbs.

The food was delicious, John couldn't believe how much he loved it. "No wonder Sophie stayed here, the food is more real than what we can get back home. There are no preservatives in anything." he said as he wiped his mouth.

"I couldn't agree more. This is great, oh, I just thought of something, we need to stay some place tonight. Let me ask for information here." Mike stood up and went over to the bar.

When he came back, he had the information he needed. "We can go to Camelot, it's a few miles down the road, there is a pub with rooms outside the castle walls. A coach comes by here in an hour, we can take that to the town."

"Great," John said, he had butterflies in his stomach. What if he ran into Sophie?

£

Kimo walked into the house first and placed some groceries on the kitchen counter. He looked out the back door, he saw his mom refilling some glasses, then he saw a dog. It hit him that he was looking at KANANI! He ran out the door and down to the beach. Kanani saw him and started barking, she ran towards him. Sophie turned and saw Kimo, then he saw Susan coming out of the house after him. Everyone was running to one hug one another. Leila followed Sophie, Kanani got to Kimo first and jumped up and licked him, he laughed. Sophie pulled Kanani off of him and hugged her friend, Susan came running down the hill too and Sophie let go of Kimo and hugged her tightly.

"I've missed both of you so much!!!" Sophie cried.

"We've missed you too!" Susan had tears of joy running down her face.

"Why are you here? What's going on?" Kimo wanted to know.

"It's too much to talk about right now, we need to talk later." Susan squeezed Sophie's hand. "I understand, we need to be careful talking so we aren't overheard, but are you ok?"

"I will be, I lost Lamorak recently." Sophie whispered.

Susan and Kimo's faces fell, "Oh no, you poor thing." Kimo hugged her.

"Dinners ready!" Kimo's mom called.

"We will talk after they go to bed." Susan said. She took Susan and Leila's hands and walked between them up to the house.

£

The next day, John and Mike had an early breakfast, then took off to look around Camelot. The village was charming to be sure. John kept looking around for any signs of Sophie but didn't see any. There was a Tournament happening in the late morning and taking place all day, so John and Mike headed over to the arena, scanning the crowd they took a seat not too far from the King and Queen. John couldn't wrap his mind around the fact that he was sitting by King Arthur! Richard looked around, he didn't see Kanani or Sophie, but he did notice a man with another German Shepherd, he thought that a bit odd, but shook it off.

Richard was walking Titus and they happened to go by the Tournament, he looked up at the people, NO! WAS THAT JOHN? He couldn't be sure, he hurried home to get Jennie. He told her what he thought he saw, and she laughed.

"Let me get changed and I'll go out with you have a look, why don't you leave Titus here and we can go watch part of the Tournament and take a look at this man." Jennie said as she put on a clean dress, "Can you get that button please?" Jennie turned and let Richard finish fastening her dress.

"There you go, turn around and let me look at you." John turned her to face him, "Gorgeous!"

Jennie kissed him, "Thanks, you don't look too bad yourself." she laughed.

"Come on, give me your arm. Titus, we will be right back." Richard took Jennie's arm and they walked out the door and over to the Tournament. When they were seated, Jennie asked Richard to point out the person he thought was John. When he did, Jennie looked at him closely. The man resembled the photos of him that Sophie had, sort of. She just wasn't sure.

"I can't be sure, but I don't think it's him, honey." Jennie said.

"Ok, I just wasn't too sure, we haven't ever met him, just seen photos from Sophie. I guess I'm just trying to see something that will comfort her." John finished saying.

"I'm not sure having John return right now would comfort her." Jennie looked at her husband sadly.

"Come on, let's go get Titus and go get dinner." Richard stood.

As they left, John glanced over at them. Jennie was a very good-looking woman, so men were always looking at her and her sister. She had dark hair, Sophie had blonde, but both were beautiful women.

Something looked familiar John thought as he looked at the good-looking woman getting up to leave with a very handsome, muscular man. It nagged him for a time. Could Sophie be here? That woman looked a bit like her, but it wasn't Sophie. John just shook his head, "Mike, let's go get a bite to eat."

"Good idea, this is fun, but I think I've seen enough for now." Mike stood and stretched. "What do you want to do? We have 12 more hours before we have to return."

"Why don't we get a bite over there, it smells good," They ordered Manchet bread with a stew, there was beef, pork, cabbage, and carrots in it, John thought it tasted delicious! Mike too, they went back and got a second helping for later that night.

"Let's walk around outside of the castle grounds and see how people live, hey! Is that a dragon?" John pointed to a giant white animal that looked very much like a dragon.

Mike laughed, "I believe it might be, but no one is running or paying any attention to it, so I don't think we are in any danger."

It was getting late, they had already checked out of the inn, so they went to a pub and sat outside, they ordered some ale and ate their stew.

"This was a nice little vacation John, it was a lot of money, but definitely worthwhile. I forgot how much fun you can be." Mike laughed.

"Very funny, it was fun for me too. I think I will go back to Hawaii with you and live there for a while, there is nothing here for me, not in Luxembourg either, I can't stay in Camelot, I don't see Sophie. She must have gone on with her life. It wouldn't be fair for me to find her, Mike." John took a long drink, then put the mug down.

"Who knows, John, Hawaii is nice, it would be good to have you fly home with me. It's your home too, you have your own suite in the hotel. I'm ready to go, are you?" Mike asked.

"Yes," John left the last of his medieval money on the table for the ale, then they left and started walking towards the portal.

£

That night Sophie and Leila sat outside with Kimo and Susan after his parents had gone to bed. Sophie told them all about the trip to L'Azure, her engagement, and the battle. It did Sophie good to be talking to her friends about this. They stayed up late and made a plan to go to Lanai, the next day. Sophie wanted to see her old market and the hotel John owned.

The next morning the four of them took the ferry over Lanai, they looked at the marina. Sophie remembered her yacht that she had lived on with Kanani and Leila.

She looked at Leila, "It brings back a lot of memories, doesn't it?"

"Yes, it does, I love my life now though, Aunt Sophie." Leila hugged her aunt.

"Me too, Leila. It's something we never could have imagined, let's check out the hotel and go home to Camelot." Sophie turned to Kimo, "Are you and Susan coming home with us?"

Kimo looked at Susan, squeezed her hand and said, "Yes, I called and we can get the flight back with you in two days' time. My folks knew we couldn't stay forever."

"Fantastic! Let's go have lunch at the hotel, then get back to Maui and spend some time with your folks." Sophie put her arm around Leila and they walked up to the hotel.

Sophie looked around, Mike was still the manager the waitress had said, but he was on vacation to England. This gave Sophie some pause. Strange, she thought, but he had made some nice changes to the hotel. In fact, this didn't used to be a restaurant, but since her cafe and market were gone, this was the only place to get lunch. It was a day well spent, and they took the last ferry back over to Maui. Two days later, Kimo's parents waved goodbye as the four of them and Kanani boarded airplane for Luxembourg.

£ JOHN AND MIKE landed back by the caves in Luxembourg, they got their clothes back out of the lockers and walked out into the sunshine.

"Well, that was quite the experience John. Too bad we didn't see Sophie, were you really looking for her or just hoping you would run into her?" Mike asked.

"I don't know, I guess I should have asked around for her, but I just couldn't. I wouldn't know what to say! We don't have anything in common anymore." John shook his head and kicked a rock with his toe. "Let's go straight to the airport, I don't even want to go back to our house, can you call a cab to take us to the airport Mike?" John asked.

Mike pulled out his cell phone, "You bet, I can't wait to get home to Hawaii and the ocean."

Unknown to either party, the planes passed one another in the air somewhere over Iceland.

£

Landing back in Luxembourg, the cab dropped all of them off at the house in Luxembourg. Sophie unlocked the door and the others went into their rooms to change. Kimo and Susan still had their own room with clothes in their closet too. No one went into the spare bedroom where John had slept. They met in the kitchen, Sophie looked around. Strange, she thought she left a phone and note for John, there was nothing here. She asked Leila about it and she didn't know anything either.

"It's like someone has been here, weird." Then Sophie went outside, there was the phone! She picked it up and went back inside.

"I found this outside!"

"Sophie, that's creepy!" Susan said.

"I didn't do it Auntie." Leila came over to look at it.

"I know, lets blame it on Kimo." Susan laughed.

Sophie laughed too, "Whew, we need to get home. Let me check the internet to see if there is anything changed about Lamorak in history." Sophie placed the phone back on the counter.

Sophie then walked into the office a got the laptop out of its case on the desk, "Wow, it's been a long time since I've been online. I'm surprised this laptop still works."

Susan walked over to her, "Yeah, a lot has changed in a couple of years. I don't think I will miss it, we didn't even get on line much in Hawaii during the time we stayed there."

"Funny how I haven't missed it either." Sophie said as she Googled, Lamorak.

"Look!"

"Lamorak was known as the third greatest knight of King Arthur's Round table. Sir Lamorak was slain by Erec, and Enide, the Orkney children of King Agravaine. Here sadly ends the journal of the great Sir Lamorak de Gales. He will be missed by his family and fiancée."

"Wow! I'm glad they didn't put my name in this article! It's so sad, I couldn't even change his history. How I loved him." Sophie sighed, Susan put her arms around Sophie's shoulders.

"I know you did, you will have another love Sophie." Susan stood, "Let's go home to Camelot tonight."

Sophie looked at her, "Yes, let's go." She closed the laptop and unplugged it, putting it back in its case. Standing Sophie looked around, she didn't want to live here, but they should keep the place. She had time to decide, the hotel in Hawaii was in a trust, so money went into a bank account here in Luxembourg, bills were now being paid automatically. There was nothing for her to worry about, time to get back to her puppy and dragon!

Gathering the others, they called a cab and were dropped off at the caves. Sophie couldn't wait to get home. She saw the booth that charged people for a trip back in time, and shook her head in disbelief. What would this world not think of? She needed to go talk to her grandpa when she returned to Camelot, she was going back to L'Azure!

TO BE CONTINUED..................

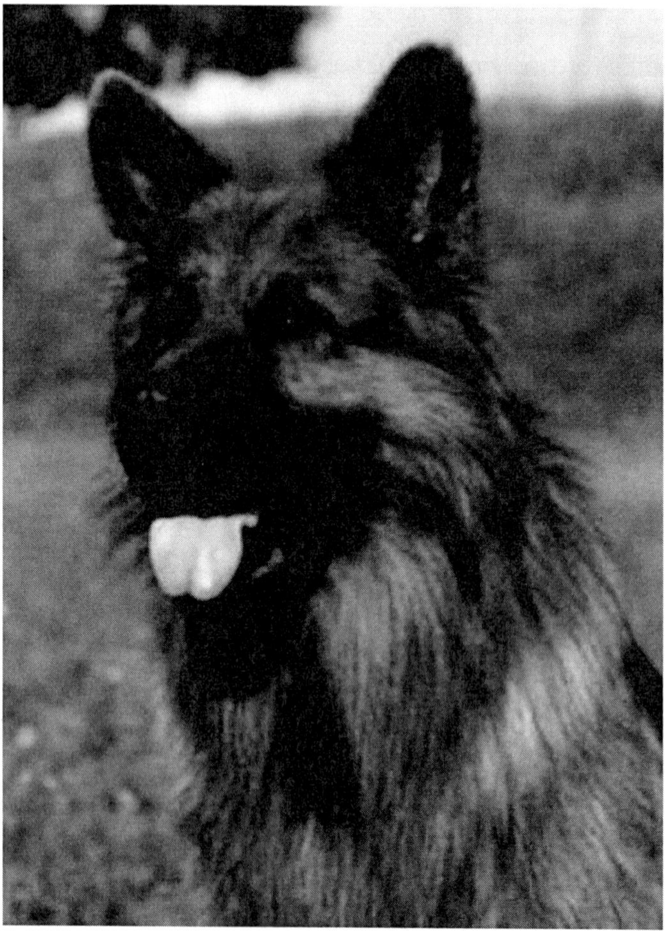

ABOUT THE AUTHOR

MICHELE WRITES UNDER the pen name of JMM Adams. She lives in the North West with her beloved German Shepherds, Horse and parrot. A new book will be out next year, it's a mystery with Casey Lane and Jackie Lee. Casey Lane finds out some dark secrets about her grandfather and in seeking the truth, she puts herself and Jackie Lee in jeopardy.

Be sure to catch all the blogs and updates on new material on Facebook under Author J.M.M. Adams, twitter and www.dragonlochworks.com

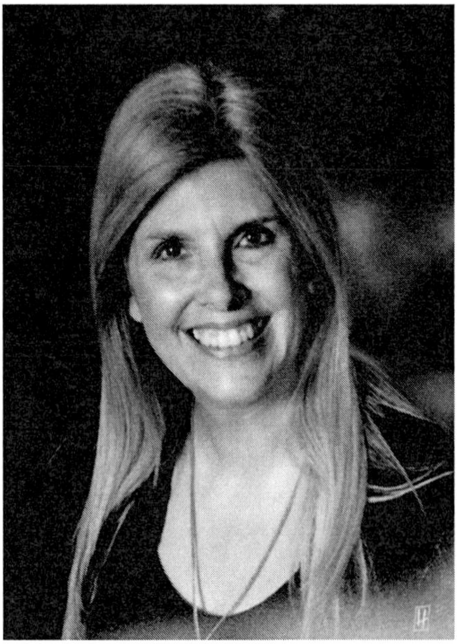

Look for the Casey Lane and Jackie Lee books, they have many mysteries to solve……..

Also, war dog hero stories coming soon. War dogs from Iraq, Kuwait and Afghanistan. A new Sophia, Gunther and perhaps the Prince of L'Azure will be out soon too.